THE ENGLISH DISEASE

THE ENGLISH
DISEASE

A NOVEL BY

JOSEPH SKIBELL

ALGONQUIN BOOKS
OF CHAPEL HILL
2003

Published by
Algonquin Books of Chapel Hill
Post Office Box 2225
Chapel Hill, North Carolina 27515-2225

a division of
Workman Publishing
708 Broadway
New York, New York 10003

Lyrics from "Anthem" by Leonard Cohen copyright © 1993 by Sony/ATV
Songs LLC. All rights administered by Sony/ATV Music Publishing, 8 Music
Square West, Nashville, TN 37203. All rights reserved. Used by permission.

Portions of this novel, in slightly different form, appeared in *Many Mountains
Moving* 2, no. 2 (1996); and *Tikkun Magazine* 18, no. 3 (2003).

This is a work of fiction. While, as in all fiction, the literary perceptions and
insights are based on experience, all names, characters, places, and incidents
are either products of the author's imagination or are used fictitiously. No
reference to any real person is intended or should be inferred. Anyone
imagining himself depicted in these pages is advised, by the author, to
consider reforming his character.

Library of Congress Cataloging-in-Publication Data
Skibell, Joseph.
        The English disease / Joseph Skibell. — 1st ed.
            p. cm.
        ISBN 1-56512-257-7
        1. Jewish men — Fiction.   2. Intellectuals — Fiction.
    3. Musicologists — Fiction.   4. Interfaith marriage — Fiction.
    5. Mahler, Gustav, 1860–1911 — Appreciation — Fiction.   I. Title.
    PS3569 K44E54 2003
    813'.54 — dc21   2003040404

10 9 8 7 6 5 4 3 2 1
First Edition

for basha ahavah, of course

באתי לגני אחתי כלה

I am thrice homeless:
as a native of Bohemia in Austria,
an an Austrian among Germans,
as a Jew throughout the world.

—GUSTAV MAHLER

Every heart
to love will come
but like a refugee.

—LEONARD COHEN

THE ENGLISH DISEASE

among dripping cacti

English melancholiacs used to tour the ruins of Antiquity as a cure for their depression, which was, in fact, at the time called the English Disease. It was thought that somehow the contemplation of actual ruins would make one's own ruined life seem less hateful, and that these dilapidated but still beautiful structures might suggest to the sensitive melancholiac the possibility of finding beauty in his own misery, indeed as essential to it.

Masturbation was a part of the English Disease, not just depression. I mention this for no particular reason. It's unclear to me how a trip, say, to Italy might effect that vice, but I imagine it has something to do with all the open piazzas.

America, too, is filled with ruins. Or the West, at least: Chaco Canyon; Mesa Verde; Betatakin, this cracked and crumbling village of stone houses, hewn into the rockface cavern of an enormous protective butte, not more than a few hundred yards long, but an entire universe, probably, for the people who once lived in it. There's little trace now of the Anasazi, according to our guide, no more than a few glyphs, a scattered collection of cliff dwellings and an astonishingly symmetrical system of roads. No one knows where they went when they left or even where they buried their dead. It's a curious fact, but there are no graves here, and it occurs to me to wonder, standing in the shadow of its broken forms, how the Anasazi treated their depression.

"Why would they be depressed, Charles, if they didn't *die?*" Isabelle says petulantly, blue eyes narrowing behind mauve lenses and I suppose she has a point, although there is *still* the masturbation problem, probably not unknown even to the unmelancholic Anasazi. And what about the Italians? it occurs to me to wonder. Surrounded on all sides by ruin and beauty, where were they sent for their depression? To Greece, it's safe to assume, plenty of ruins there, all of civilization's, in fact, but at least they knew where their dead were buried, which is more than I can say for myself. My ancestors' bones are probably on exhibit in some Holocaust museum deep in the Polish countryside.

Now, there's a depressing thought and I can't help scowling at Isabelle. How stupid to think a trip out West could save our marriage.

AFTER NEARLY THREE quarters of an hour, the tour guide is ready to leave the ancient village. It's a long walk up to the parking lot in the blistering Arizona sun. Hurrying only makes it worse, and yet I can't seem to help myself. In front of me, a tall man, his hands carefully placed upon his hips, ascends the endless stone staircase slowly in what looks like perfect, rapturous calm. His chin is square, enormous. He calls out in Swiss German to his children, who scamper and scurry like rugged goats up and down the bleached stone switchback.

"Probably nothin' compared to the mountains in their backyard, yuh?" a fellow struggler says to me between puffs of heated air.

I permit myself a smile, albeit a peevish one.

It's unbearable, this heat, and I have no wish to be jollied or insinuated into this man's misery-loving company. I've lost sight now of Isabelle. I don't know where she is or even if she's behind or in front of me. I feel an urgent need to punish her for everything that is happening, including the fact that I don't know where she is so that I can't, and the indecision over whether to hurry the rest of the way up or to wait for her here so that I may upbraid her immediately only makes the walk more and more unpleasant. She's not in the rickety old school bus they brought us in from the ranger station; I see that as soon as I emerge over the plateau line into the dirt lot. I refuse to descend again in order to meet her coming up, and I wait, instead, seething, inside the bus, without ventilation, surrounded by these happy Swiss, so obnoxious in their indifference to the misery all around them.

When Isabelle finally arrives, she's accompanying an elderly couple who gibber incoherently, half-scalded out of their minds with probable sunstroke. The old man's pate is boiled a violent lobster red. His bewildered wife searches idiotically through her handbag for the car keys she will not, until later, need. Isabelle helps them to a seat and takes her place beside me. Neither of us speaks, although she can't help grasping my arm when the bus, at full speeds, trundles down the winding mountain road, edging impossibly close to the drop-off. She whispers "*Stop!*" and "*Please stop!*" involuntarily towards the back of the driver, who couldn't hear her over the bus's rumble even if she shouted at him in full voice, as she has done so often lately at me.

I can't help being further annoyed.

She's the one who insisted on this trip.

WOMEN HAVE ALWAYS been the source of my greatest unhappiness, beginning with Alma Mahler and my researches into her husband Gustav's life when I was but a graduate student. Isabelle says I'm wrong to take it personally, but how could she have slept with the architect Gropius and all the others while her husband, music's most melancholic genius, was slowly and painfully dying, transforming whatever was left of his life into the late magisterial works?

This is not a situation with which I am altogether unfamiliar. At least by analogy. I don't compare myself to Mahler, but the night before I was to defend my dissertation on the Second Symphony, for instance, I found my then-girlfriend in bed with her roommate, an alluring woman I myself had at one time considered stepping outside of the relationship to approach. None of their well-meaning excuses, nothing they said, could, the next day, erase from my mind, the horrifyingly indelible picture of the two of them devouring each other on her stained futon, their four full breasts corseted tightly against their twin abdomens, as I sat before my doctoral committee. Happily, I passed; but then, not more than two years later, with my first extended monograph, *Neuroticism and the Opening Heart in the Song Cycles of Gustav Mahler,* accepted for publication, my editor at the university press, an unstable woman that even people with no interest in my work had warned me against, disappeared for five agonizing weeks with the only complete copy of the text. Later, she revealed to me that upon arrival in Montréal for a professional conference, she had given in to an overwhelming need to scour the Canadian border towns in search of the child she'd been forced, as a troubled and unmarried teenager in Ottawa, to surrender up for adoption. Hot on the trail, she had simply forgotten that she had brought along the manuscript to proof, and now, reasonable again and returned to the States and to a somewhat more drastic dosage of Lithium, she felt it was only a matter of time before she might recall, with any clarity, the name of the motel in which it had been left.

(The manuscript, unlike the child, was never located. I see him sometimes around the department, an awkward adolescent, nervous like his mother.)

There were other women, of course, as my life and career progressed, each, it seemed, with her own portion of my heart to break, until at last I met Isabelle and fell in love with her out of exhaustion, more than anything else. This isn't true, of course. She was catering a faculty recital the first time I saw her, and despite a debilitating migraine, I couldn't help following her into the kitchen and speaking to her there. Even through the patterned distortions in my visual field (a common migraine symptom), her beauty was alarming. Everything about her seemed blonde. She had large, blonde hands, blonde skin, eyes that were blue, of course, actually, but which were impossible for me, when I conjured her face on the grey walls of my office, to imagine as anything other than blonde.

Her clothes were blonde, and her apartment, or at least its furnishings, which were principally of varnished pine.

I would awaken in the middle of the night, sunken deep in the overstuffed comforters of her bed, and gaze at the long blonde dunes of her body shimmering in the moonlight like a vast expanse of Mediterranean beach in which I had temporarily lost my way. Together, we huddled beneath her sheets, and in the morning, I sat at her wobbly breakfast table and watched her move through her small kitchen like a glistening refraction of golden light, brightening everything she touched, including (most palpably) my own dour moods, which assailed me at a less severe frequency than at any other time I could easily recall.

Isabelle forgave me my sadnesses, my habitual cynicism, and my tendency to speak to her as though I were refuting an accusation made by a rival's hostile claque.

Now, WHENEVER ISABELLE is angry, she brings up Gustav Mahler.

True, it's a fact that before they were married, he forbade Alma to continue on with her own compositions, refusing to marry her otherwise, but I've never understood what this has got to do with me, or with Isabelle, for that matter. We are probably the only people in the entire Southwest discussing the subject at the moment, certainly the only two campers in all of Canyonlands who even know who Gustav Mahler is or was.

It's not exactly the sort of conversation by which one usually pitches a tent.

This current assault on poor Gustav (who, let us remember, had problems of his own) began shortly after we pulled out of the Navajo National Monument and has increased steadily in animus the farther we've driven north into Utah.

And what can one say?

Mahler was a neurotic, granted; an egoist, and a depressive

in frail health. It was a different age; men thought of women differently.

Useless to point out that his young wife accepted and stuck to the terms of this idiosyncratic agreement while flagrantly disregarding the weightier ones of her marriage vow. Is it really possible that a woman who would think nothing of sleeping with half of fin de siècle Vienna, who had the ingenuity to stage-manage, well into the twentieth century, a complicated rotation of transatlantic trysts and assignations, couldn't find a quiet hour away from a busy husband and her two already neglected children to clandestinely compose?

"But composition is not supposed to be a clandestine activity, Charles!" Isabelle nearly screams this, and her voice resounds throughout the deserted canyons. "Infidelity *by its very nature* is. Comparing the two is totally unfair!"

The tension we've been feeling reaches its breaking point and we very nearly come to physical blows over the collapsible tent spines. Neither of us, at this moment, can believe that the other knows anything about constructing a tent. Fortunately, the metal spikes are too dull to pierce skin or else the temptation to stab one another might prove overwhelming. It's absurd, this petty little war of ours, waged in a landscape as vast and empty as the Heavens. Canyonlands, for those of you who have never seen it, looks like nothing so much as a life-size version of one of those castle-like candle sculptures hippies used to sell in head shops when I was a boy and that are once again popular, those flowing, overcomplicated fire hazards whose architects must have conceived of them through a psilocybinic haze and which Cloud (her real name Marjorie), fetching in a tie-dyed nightshirt, always lit on the bookshelf above her bed the summer I relaxed my strict prohibition against dating any of my students. Its sloping rock hills are a porous limestone called tufa, remarkably facile for climbing, and I'm aware of an impulse to walk out of my marriage by ascending the steep rock wall we've pitched our little green tent against, continuing to the highest peaks, ignoring Isabelle's regret-filled cries, and vaulting into the Empyrean like the biblical Enoch, although Enoch probably—almost certainly—wasn't running from his wife.

"You can be sure if Mahler had had affairs," Isabelle presses the point, "they would have been clandestine!"

She ties down a portion of the tent guard.

"But he didn't, Isabelle, did he?"

"No?" she says. "And why not?"

"Because how could he?" I say. "He was too depressed over Alma for one thing!"

"That's *not* the point I'm making, Charles. That is *not* my point and you know it!"

"And have I asked you to stop composing?" I say boldly in my own defense, immediately aware of how stupid it sounds.

"I'm not a composer, Charles."

Needlessly, she reminds me of this.

"Or whatever your analogy is."

"My analogy? My analogy is that I just follow you around, blindly doing whatever you want to do, never asking myself what I want to do, so that we never, in fact, do any of the things I want!"

"Like what?" I say, although I regret it immediately.

It's no use asking Isabelle for specific examples. She's too good at throwing them in your face.

"You didn't want to take this trip, for instance!"

"Because I hate to travel, Isabelle, and you know that!"

"Oh—oh and right—and I'm just supposed to live without it then?"

"But you're not. Look around you!" I say. "We're traveling. *I'm* the one who's miserable!"

"Yes and making sure I don't enjoy a minute of it. . . ."

We continue on this way as the afternoon grows short and our tent is completed and our pillows and our mats and our sleeping bags and everything else, including ourselves—("Don't you *dare* touch me!" Isabelle screams)—have been thrown in through its open flap. Inside, we sit on the small hillocks of our sleeping bags, our faces closer than they've been in weeks, pressed together now not by the sensual impulsion of a kiss, rather by the narrowing apex of the canvas sheeting. At this range, so near, I can't ignore the anger traveling visibly across Isabelle's features, darkening her normally placid face.

All this talk about Alma Mahler—even after all these years, she's still breaking hearts!—but what could Isabelle have meant by it? Usually she has no patience for the trivialities associated with my work: poor ailing Gustav; his heartless, unfaithful Alma.

Why, suddenly, so spirited a defense?

It's as though someone, a djinn, had breathed the words into my ear. Certain pointed questions uncurl themselves inside my brain: Has she taken a lover? I wonder. Is that what this is all about? Is she seeing someone behind my back?

These unpleasant thoughts announce themselves as the first light taps of rain, hitting the tent, break into our concentrated animosities. A gigantic thunderclap follows and, instantly, before either of us can say another word, the tent begins to fill with water. I unzip the opaque flap and, through the transparent screening, see a river of rainwater coursing down the rockface and covering the small plateau upon which we've constructed our little tent.

There is nothing else to do.

I jump through the flap into the downpour, followed by the whirring murmur of lightning-quick zippers as Isabelle seals herself in behind me. The water is already almost an inch above the tent bottom and, on my knees and soaking wet, I dig a moat by hand into the softened reddish loam, encircling the tent like some medieval king, protecting his wife and castle, but too late, from invaders.

My circle complete, I stand on the far shore of the muddle, a wet and silent figure among the dripping cacti.

a momentary break in the rain

The momentary break in the rain lasts only long enough for the two of us to repack our things into the tiny trunk of Isabelle's car before the sky darkens and it all starts up again: Grey, thick and heavy sheets, impossible to pilot a car through, although Isabelle seems to be enjoying herself and even managing quite well. This is the sort of thing she loves most, I know—an adventure!—and so I let her drive. Neither of us really trusts me behind the wheel anyway: she, because of the storms; myself, because I'm too enraged and depressed to even speak.

Who is it? who is it? who?

I stare out the window and imagine what the slides of this trip might have looked like had either Isabelle or I thought to bring along a camera: *Here we are at the Navajo National Monument where Isabelle confided to me that she has been sleeping with X.* (Who is it? who is it? who?) *Here I am, wandering off into the cliffs, an abject and forlorn figure.* (Who? who? who?) *This is me, weeks later, unshaven and in rags, disguising my voice by placing a weathered kerchief across the mouthpiece of a dusty pay phone* ("Who is this?") *luring an unsuspecting X out into the desert, where I pummel him to death with a Coleman lantern before burying his body in various out-of-the-way places—there's a whole series of these, with the coyotes yipping and an owl hooting.* (Who! who! who!) *And in this final photograph, as you can see, I'm turning myself in at the ranger's station, it's dark and the focus is no good, so you can't really make out the look of remorse on my face, but I tell you, it's there, it's there, it's there . . .*

"But Charles," *my friends will surely say above the humming slide projector,* "you always look like that."

" *CHARLES!* " ISABELLE'S VOICE cuts through my mental screen like a heart surgeon snipping at a patient's aorta. "We have to stop," she says.

I recognize only too well the tone of finality in her voice.

"I know, I know," I say, and inwardly, I prepare myself for the worst.

"It's too dangerous," she says, and of course she's right. I don't understand the first thing about adultery. Even as a child, I misunderstood the word, thinking it described not an act of illicit fornication, but rather the process of growing up, something the Seventh Commandment inexplicably forbade.

THOU SHALT NOT GROW UP—I AM THE LORD THY GOD!

It's a strange word, *adultery*. Whispering inside its *d* and its *t* is its own disapproving tut-tut. *A(tut-tut)ery*.

I look up at the sky. Large purple and black clouds have gathered into big fists above the road, casting an eerie lavender light.

Isabelle checks her mirrors. Biting her lower lip, she steers with difficulty through the rain. Her arms, as stiff as oars against the wheel, extend through the sockets of her sleeveless denim blouse, the pucker of her vaccination mark visible beneath the down of her arm. I sit next to her, exiled from her usually generous affections, and near enough to smell the pleasant scent of rain upon her skin.

"All right, that's it!" she screams as a red pickup truck whooshes past us, raising in its wake a flood of water that covers our windshield like a grey, liquid quilt. Isabelle's thumbs redden against the buttons of the horn. My hands flail about as I attempt to protect myself uselessly inside the knots of my crossed arms and crossed legs.

"I-I-I-I-I," I stammer.

"We're pulling off!" she says, and I can only nod as she steers the car from the road into a soggy dirt lot.

hole n" the rock

Isabelle shifts into neutral, allowing the motor to idle. She shivers and, with two hands, rubs the bare skin of her thighs. Gripping the hem of her cotton shirt into her fist, she rubs the condensation from her window in large, violent circles. The glass squeaks. Craning my neck for a better view through the wipers' shimmy, I see an enormous red butte with a series of aluminum partitions built into the bottom third of its rough wall, more the sort of thing you'd see on a mobile home or a hunting lodge, each partition shaped like a half-buried moon with windows and screens and uninspired filigree. In the center partition is a screen door, and above it, across the rockface, are the words

HOLE N" THE ROCK spelled out in dirty white letters. Twelve feet above the sign and far to its right, in a recessed niche, is a granite bust that looks like Franklin Delano Roosevelt might have if he'd been someone who only vaguely resembled himself. A collection of cars and trucks are clustered together in the dirt lot. A handwritten sign on the door says OPEN.

Isabelle and I contemplate each other across the car roof, our bodies half inside the doors on either side, each reluctant to commit an afternoon to this godforsaken place.

And yet what else are we to do?

It's raining; it's impossible to drive farther; we're tourists, after all, a married couple on holiday out West; and another hour trapped inside Isabelle's Volkswagen Rabbit will do neither of us any good.

And so: without discussion or further thought, we dash horizontally through the vertical drizzle into what another sign (this one on wheels by the roadside with blinking orange lights and flashing arrows) reiterates is HOLE N" THE ROCK — AS SEEN ON NATIONAL TV!

INSIDE, WE'RE GREETED by a young girl with a light mask of pimples on her chin and a green polyester turtleneck across her throat. She introduces herself to us as our guide in a nasal sing-song, from whose monotonous rhythms she will not deviate for the next half-hour or so. Or perhaps for the rest of her life. Still, it's good to be in the dry though musty foyer. With its counter and its sofa and its sign-in registry, it resembles the offices of a cheap motel. A half-dozen other visitors mill about, thick-girthed men in farm caps and jeans. Their wives are plump in brightly patterned costumes, pants with big stretch-waists, burgundy, turquoise and cream in color, their arms dangling out of their striped short sleeves like albino salamis.

They have traveled, some of them (I can't help overhearing this), great distances expressly for the purpose of being here.

"We saw't on that television show t'other night?" one of them says.

"Oh yes and we planned for it all summer."

"It was out of our way, 'course, but we wun't have missed it for the world."

"Christ!" I say and Isabelle nudges me for it in the ribs. It's a small threat, but also the first time she's touched me voluntarily in weeks. I'm miserable, knowing that my marriage is ending and that I'm helpless to prevent it. I glance surreptitiously at Isabelle. She's the only woman here who could be described as even remotely attractive, the only one with any intelligence in her eyes.

The others all resemble those Russian dolls that fit one inside the other.

• • •

Our guide asks the eight or so of us to please follow her, leading us down a narrow, crooked passageway. In line with the others, I'm beginning to experience the first stirrings of claustrophobic panic. There is neither light nor space here, and a large man inadvertently steps upon my heel, causing the canvas to slide beneath my foot.

"Ooomps, sorry," he says, regaining his step as our line moves forward.

Unable to stop, I'm forced to limp, rotating my ankle in an attempt to restore my foot to its proper place inside the shoe, lifting one leg and hopping, pulling out the canvas with my finger, until the man bumps into me again, stepping on my other foot and, this time, although the shoe remains in place, his heavy boot breaks the skin over my tendon.

Walking backwards before us, our guide describes, in her dulling drawl, how the man who built Hole N" The Rock had dreamed, since childhood, of living beneath the surface of the earth, something from which his family naturally tried to dissuade him.

"But then," she says brightly, "his mother died and in her will she left him"—I can't believe I'm hearing this correctly—"a mule, a cache of dynamite and a small plot of land. This was during the Great Depression," she tells us—hence, the high regard for FDR—"and with no job and little else to occupy his time"— plus, all the necessary equipment, I think—"Albert"—at last, I catch his name—"decided to make his lifelong dream come true."

She stops before a sealed door and our line stops obediently, if raggedly, before her.

"Working countless backbreaking hours," she continues in her marked twang, "in mourning for his mom, and with only the help of his trusting mule Harry, young Albert Christensen built his dream house right into the bosom of the earth and not too far from Moab."

Although I myself had considered flying off the tufa into the Heavens, it never occurred to me to live, like a lizard, beneath the rocks, and I find the idea completely without appeal.

Our guide opens the door and our little group, gasping for air, pushes through it into the cave's main living room. Spinning in circles like Sufis, we take in what is essentially a tasteless crackerbox, circa 1938, except (here, as one, our group looks up) its ceilings and walls are cave rock, there is no yard to keep, no neighbors to bother with, and no natural light of any kind.

To make matters worse, Albert and his wife (can her name really have been Gladys?) filled their subterranean bungalow with an unfortunate number of homemade things, including, I see around the first corner, Albert's amateur paintings of Jesus and the Apostles, all with bulging apoplectic eyes (Our guide: "Displayed here for your enjoyment"), and various other scenes of religious significance.

"Oooh!" the crowd marvels.

"So real!" someone says.

"Yes and they certainly do follow you around the room, don't they?"

"He could heal lepers and effect resurrections," I whisper to Isabelle, "and yet his own thyroid troubles somehow eluded him."

"Ssshh!" she shushes me, and the hissing sound, reverberating against the dense walls, returns to us, embarrassing us both. The others in our party seem to be doing their best to ignore us as we trudge dutifully along together, a shambling behemoth, the shuffling of our many feet muffled inside these cavernous halls.

"And here," the guide says with a flourish of her pale, nail-bitten hand, "is what we at Hole N" The Rock like to call the Underground Love Grotto."

She stands before a hollowed-out den, Gladys' bedroom, it would seem, inside of which is a bed on a raised platform, its homemade yo-yo quilt covered by an army of fiendish-looking ragdolls, crafts-fair monstrosities, so fiercely deformed they would give a normal person nightmares.

"She loved these dolls," our guide says, sucking on the rim of her turtleneck, staining the fabric of its collar with a wet impression of her teeth. "This was her bed. And she kept her dolls here."

The monotonous intervals of her speech, a minor seventh repeated and repeated before descending to the tonic, have begun to grate on my nerves. When I look at our crowd of gawking bumpkins, however, none of them seems bothered by it in the least.

Instead, "Impressive," one woman says to her husband, eyeing the dolls.

"There are so many of them!" gushes another.

"They probably kept Albert and the mule out of her bed, don't you think?" I mutter.

Isabelle folds her arms across her chest and gives me a stern look, and yet I think I see that she is laughing, at least a little bit, beneath it.

WE ARE MOVED swiftly into the den, given over almost entirely to an exhibition of Albert's ill-starred attempts at taxidermy. Various now amorphous animals seem to leap and dance from every nook and cranny like wildlife amoebas. The centerpiece here is the beloved mule himself, which predeceased Albert. Albert, it seems, couldn't stand to be parted from the mule, not after all they'd been through, and so he's stuffed, mid-buck, in a sort of boneless bronco pose, a large zipperlike stitch visible down the humpy center of his back.

I half-expect to find Gladys in a similar position in another corner of the room, and say as much to Isabelle.

BY THE TIME we reach the Desert Gem Room, the final stop on our tour, neither she nor I can stop laughing—openly, raucously, in big plosive bursts that seem to carom, amplified, off the cave walls.

"Sshhh!"

"Shush!"

"Hush, y'all!" a few in our party hiss at us, but most of them, I notice, simply avoid looking in our direction, out of an honest compassion, I suspect, pitying us for the lack of some essential quality which prevents us from experiencing the place with appropriate reverence.

On the contrary: Isabelle is doubled over and in spasms, and our guide must raise her already straining voice to explain above our insensitive chortlings that in this room, ("an ordinary workroom with a long wooden table on its humble dirt floor,") Gladys spent the afternoons of her life sanding down and polishing ordinary rocks and stones until they shone like desert gems, which she'd sell as curios to curious tourists, such as ourselves.

"The most popular of these so-called desert gems," our guide warbles nasally, "was made out of . . . that's right, you've guessed it," she says, although no one has, "ordinary Coke bottles found alongside the road."

The crowd sighs in astonished pleasure. Isabelle giggles, clutching my arm and expecting me to laugh as well, but I don't. I can't. It's difficult to explain, but something in the story depresses me, and a sense of despair seems to shake me from within. My legs buckle and, in an instant, I'm on my knees and weeping, holding my rib cage and wailing, breathing with difficulty through my sobs, as the others stand in a concerned circle above me. Through tears, I see that several of them are also weeping. They seem to exhibit none of the derision I would have expected from them and which I would have shown to any one of their number, I'm certain, were he in my place and I in his.

This stark confirmation of my own callousness only makes me weep more. I pull in hard breaths. An acrid lump burns inside my throat. I can't seem to find my voice and, instead, gesture uselessly towards the others with my hands, my signaling incomprehensible, even to myself.

Finally, Isabelle steps forward. Never has she looked so tender or so caring, her face alive with a compassion I see reflected on all the other faces encircling me. Luminous in the dark cave light, she holds out her arms to me and bends, whispering in my ear.

"Let's get out of here, okay, sweetie?"

My weeping subsides, and the others are able to help me to my feet. There is little talk and perhaps one or two tentative, sympathetic hugs, but the tour is definitely over.

I THANK OUR GUIDE near the exit as quickly as possible, avoiding her eyes, too embarrassed, really, to look into them until she takes my hand and shakes it warmly.

"You'd be surprised how often I seen this same thing happen," she tells me.

"Is that right?" Isabelle asks her.

"Yes, ma'am," she says before turning to the last crush of tourists for the day.

Our small group emerges from beneath the earth into the rain-filtered light, into the heavy liquid air. We head for our separate cars. Isabelle opens the door for me. She slips into the driver's seat and throws her purse into the back, the blonde streak of her bare arm arching in a curving flash. She maneuvers the gearshift, an old crone tapping a cane, and then sits up straight, locking a loose strand of hair behind her ear, as though she were a schoolgirl.

(In this instant, sitting beside her, it's as though I've seen the entire continuum of her existence.)

She points the car towards Moab, the road ringing with rain.

The sun falls behind the reddened earth.

"S'whew!" she says.

And, "Hey?"

She laughs to herself and, looking sideways at me, says, "Belski, man . . . I mean, what happened to you in there?"

myth of the eternal return

There are, I suppose, many explanations for what happened to me inside the caves at Hole N" The Rock, although none of them are particularly satisfying. At least not to me. Still, Isabelle seems intrigued by her own theories. "Hunh," is all I can say, not really wanting to hear them, as she prattles on about landscape and its relationship to psyche, caves and their womblike structures, the uroboric earth vomiting me out like a newborn child.

It is all I can do, in fact, to remove my glasses and pinch the bridge of my nose as tightly as possible, while she drones on and on about Mircea Eliade, whose *Myth of the Eternal Return* had been a significant text for her during an unhappy semester-and-a-half as a graduate student in religious studies shortly before she divorced her first husband. That he was rumored to have been a fascist ideologue and a Nazi sympathizer distresses her still. (I mean Eliade, of course, and not Isabelle's first husband.) And though I tried to reason with her, she was similarly distressed when Joseph Campbell was exposed as an antisemite and also when Cat Stevens, whose peace- and love-filled songs had been a guiding star for her as a teenager, announced his support, as a Muslim convert, for the fatwa against Salman Rushdie.

Such political reprehensibility is hardly remarkable, I argued. Why, the cultural pantheon of the West is filled with figures whose political leanings and petit bourgeois prejudices make them suspect at best. Not only Wagner, of course, but also Marx, Heidegger, Pound, Jung, Eliot, Genet, Luther, Voltaire, Erasmus, Saints Ambrose and John Chrysostom, Heisenberg, Conrad, Dostoyevsky, Céline, the list goes on and on, all of them antisemitic, of course, and most of them romantically deluded proponents of violence and its redemptive power.

"Look beneath the wheel of any revolution," as my grandfather used to say, "and you'll find the body of a trampled Jew!"

"Well, that may be, Charles, that may very well be"—Isabelle pushes aside my finger, which I have inadvertently pointed at her chest—"but it's really beside the point, isn't it?"

"Is it?" I say, replacing my glasses and glaring at her, newly in focus.

(She still can't listen to *Tea for the Tillerman*.)

"Every time you have an unguarded moment—I mean, my God, Charles—somehow all of Western civilization is to blame!"

"Hole N" The Rock is hardly the caves at Lascaux, if that's what you're insin——"

"No, no, but the effects on your psyche—"

"Oh, Isabelle, please!"

"—are probably similar—*yes!*—to what initiates in those caves felt millennia ago and will you please just *stop* laughing at me!"

She sighs.

"In any case," she says, "you know you're just using this whole thing to avoid the subject of—"

"Of children?"

"Of children, yes, Charles. Bravo! You've said it yourself."

She's not difficult to anticipate. Lately, all her conversational roads lead to this single Rome, all her thoughts hie, like pilgrims, to this solitary Mecca.

"You agreed we'd discuss it on this trip."

"We agreed to discuss it, yes, but not to consider it. We've considered it already, Isabelle, and we've already agreed."

And yet, to my chagrin, the issue of children remains a sore point between us. And it's my fault, really. Recklessly, I'd insisted upon making childlessness a condition of our marriage, albeit one to which Isabelle had, if reluctantly, agreed. Children, I argued, would only interfere with our lives and our work.

"And with your own pathetic childhood!" she had screamed. "Which is *permanently* and *pathetically* ongoing!"

(She can be quite harsh at times, and needlessly cruel.)

And yet, despite my own (granted: occasional) misgivings, I continued to consider the agreement a governing principle of our union, resisting not only my own at times faltering resolve, but also Isabelle's guerilla-like attempts to topple it, examples of which I will, out of modesty, spare you, my dear reader, except to say that Isabelle is not an unattractive woman, neither is she without guile, and many a night, like the virgin Scheherazade, I managed to survive by my wit alone.

EVEN WITHOUT CHILDREN, marriage was nothing I ever wanted. Isabelle, on the other hand, although she will not admit it, had been, like all women, although they will not admit it, single-minded in her pursuit of marriage.

It was as though marriage were a marathon for which she'd trained her entire life, or if not a marathon, then a multigenerational relay race, begun in the earliest mists of prehistory and run, in an endless chain, mother to daughter, mother to daughter, and I, like all men before me, only the latest in a series of interchangeable batons.

It's not the same for a man, of course. The metaphors are different.

Although a man may feel the absence of love as an unendurable privation, the moment a woman advances, like a redemptive army, into his life, the liberating effects of the revolution she occasions begin to pale, and love becomes as oppressive as any colonizing power.

And what are children, I ask you, except an attempt by a woman, as though she were in fact a colonial regime, to erect a monument to herself on the very land she has conquered in order to remind the natives there of the civilizing advances she has brought them, when all they really want (like any man) is to have their autonomy returned?

Also: people who want children tend, I've noticed, to misremember their own childhood, recalling it as an impossibly radiant and far-horizoned garden from which they've been more or less tragically exiled, and Isabelle, unfortunately, is one of these. To hear her carrying on, nearly rhapsodic, over late-night gatherings at her grandmother's house on Mosholu Avenue where the rugs were literally rolled up so that her immigrant grandparents and their American-born children, her aunts and uncles, might jig the night away—the men in shirtsleeves and ties, their heads pressed together, crooning old ballads in the kitchen, the ice in their whiskeys tinkling, the women, flushed and exhausted, having danced themselves into states of delicious delirium, chattering away now in chairs, their cheeks high and red, gossiping in the living room, while Isabelle and her sister Oona, hidden away on the staircase, listen in their pajamas to the sounds these adults make, a roaring hum punctuated by an occasional gatling burst of laughter—you'd think she'd grown up in a sentimental storybook, a secret Irish garden, never mind her mother's drunken tyranny or her father's ability to devastate them all by disappearing first from their lives and then from life itself without warning.

(Having checked himself out of the psychiatric ward of the VA, he walked into traffic on North Broadway and was struck by a car whose driver bore the improbably Arthurian name of Perceival Gilchrist.)

"It's the only *real* time, childhood, don't you think?" Isabelle said to me one morning, staring into space in our little breakfast nook, her chin cradled against her long fingers. "Or don't you feel that, Belski?"

What I felt at that moment was only how unnerving was this habit she has of dropping philosophically leaden comments into her conversation, as though they were cubes of sugar into her breakfast tea, and besides, I'd never felt that way. On the contrary, I'd been only too eager to escape the confinement of my own childhood. My DNA having been cooked for over a thousand years in preparation for a Jewish life in Eastern Europe, it was something of a shock to wake up newly born in Karkel, Texas, with its tumbleweeds and its dusty plains, its occasionally cowboy-hatted schoolchildren and its tap water so highly fluoridated it mottled the teeth of children who didn't drink bottled water a snotty yellow-green.

Why Isabelle wished to force another innocent child through the flaming hogheads of life's humiliating circus was as mysterious to me as had been her desire to marry in the first place.

As far as I was concerned, we'd been happy enough living independently together for nearly seven years, two solitaries, more or less on equal footing, before Isabelle began this gynæcic quest of hers, haranguing me so frequently about the necessity of marriage that finally one evening, simply to change the subject, I stupidly attempted to mollify her by saying, "Perhaps this year, Isabelle, who knows?"

"This year, Charles? Do you really mean it?"

"We'll see, we'll see."

"Oh, but do you really mean it?" she said.

And although we both knew that I hadn't, she began making her plans, little by little at first, then gradually more and more, until finally she suggested, since I had in fact proposed, when in fact we both knew that I hadn't, that we marry in London the following spring, where I was going for a conference on Mahler anyway.

By this point, she'd been turned down by a scad of rabbis and was feeling blistered by my parents as well. My father, a furrier by trade, advised me to "Put her into cold storage, Charlie," while my mother, dying from an undiagnosed case of lymphoma, seemed to possess the prescience of the doomed: "You're not letting her force you into this, are you, darling?"

By marrying abroad in a brief civil ceremony, Isabelle reasoned publicly, we could avoid not only the expense of a formal wedding but any further variations on these religious and familial strains.

More: privately embarrassed by what we both knew was my own fainthearted acquiescence to her more determined will, she no doubt believed that by marrying in front of strangers, in a foreign country, thousands of miles from anyone who knew us, we might minimize the feelings of resentment and estrangement a wedding would occasion, for differing reasons, in each of us.

giving false information to the registrar

The registrar in London, however, refused to permit it.

A dignified man, his grey-black hair brushed forward across his forehead, his mustaches new and springy after their morning wash, he was courteous in a fussy British way, politely soft-spoken and mildly confused, even slightly chagrined perhaps by this American couple who sat before him, the woman straight up and leaning eagerly forward, the man slumped miserably in his chair.

It was quite early and we were clearly his first appointment for the day.

After seating himself behind his desk, he took a moment to collect his papers and then patiently explained to us that there was, in fact, a two-week residency requirement for foreign couples wishing to marry in England.

He asked us if we were, indeed, planning on staying in London for two weeks, and he was sitting in front of a sign that read

GIVING FALSE INFORMATION

TO THE REGISTRAR

IS

PERJURY!

and the word PERJURY! was in extra-large letters followed by a drastic exclamation point.

Although we were, in fact, scheduled to cross the channel for Ireland that very morning, heedless Americans that we were, we told him that, of course, we had arranged to stay. And this wasn't far from the truth. After a nine-day trip to Ireland, we were planning on returning to England, not only for my conference but for further travels, all before the two weeks were out.

England, Ireland, what difference did it make?

Had I not already disregarded not only the wishes of my family, but also, as my father kept reminding me, the theocentrifugal laws of our people and therefore, one might presume, if one were so inclined, the dictates of my Creator?

Under these circumstances, who really gave a fuck about the Queen?

The answer to that question was, of course, the registrar. He jotted down the phone number and the address of the B&B we had checked out of an hour before, and which—as though her integrity were at stake, Isabelle always maintains at this point whenever *she* tells this story—we were scheduled to recheck into only nine days later, and, after another polite question or two, he politely excused himself from the room.

One might have thought, in the wake of one disastrous marriage, that Isabelle would be leery about the entire enterprise, but the opposite was true. She seemed radiant and blushing in the registrar's office, already a bride, as we sat in our uncomfortable chairs, both of us glancing periodically at the GIVING FALSE INFORMATION TO THE REGISTRAR IS PERJURY! sign behind his desk, Isabelle fiddling with her watch, concerned that if he took much longer we would miss our boat, a fact which, because she could not mention it to him, only frustrated her more.

I, on the other hand, felt sick to my stomach, partially the result of the typically English breakfast of gelatinous eggs and anhydric toast we had shared, partially of this preposterous wedding hanging, like a guillotine, above my head. Like a condemned man asked to appreciate the beauty of the landscape between his cell and the gallows, I'd been incapable of enjoying even a minute of the trip. It wasn't so much that I despised Isabelle for needing the bourgeois reassurances of a formal wedding contract—although I did despise her and precisely for this—it was worse: I hated myself for my ridiculously puerile responses to her needs.

Gallows! Guillotines! Death sentences!

How could I be so childish? I was a grown man, after all, with agency and free will. Why on earth was I allowing a woman *half my size* to force me into marrying her, when in truth, as I've said, I'd never imagined myself married at all?

No, instead (as I would realize only later) I'd been laboring under a gross misapprehension concerning who I actually was. Somehow, I had persuaded myself, contrary to all the evidence, that I was a free-spirited Lothario, if not polygamous, then se-rially monogamous, involving myself in one brief and intense love affair after the next, my heart and groin, those twin organs of desire, chaffed in deferent service each to the other, while, in fact, I was more like one of those sad uncles out of Chekhov, sexless and long past romance well before the age of forty.

The registrar returned to his office and coughed an embarrassed cough. "You realize," he said, "that at least one of you must re-main consistently at a local address for a minimum of two weeks." He was polite, but he was politely calling us liars.

Or worse: PERJURERS!

And we could have been offended, although I, for one, cer-tainly wasn't. I can't speak for Isabelle, but at that moment I felt only an intense gratitude towards this stuffy, small-minded bureaucrat whose pedantic adherence to the finer points of phar-isaical governance had frustrated Isabelle's designs while confirm-ing my own internally enunciated suspicions that marriage, at least in a civilized country like England, was in fact a crime.

He bid us good morning and, like an American rube, I

pumped his hand too wildly as I thanked him for his time. As we stepped out onto Marylebone Road, with its diesel buses and its drab municipal buildings, its grey pigeons and its bleary skies, England never looked so beautiful. Isabelle was once again her winning self, my heart's companion, my lover and a friend. And because she never again mentioned marriage in the course of the many long and sweet conversations we shared over the remainder of our trip, dawdling over coffee or strolling through museums or hiking the countryside, I allowed myself to assume that habit, overtaking us, had reasserted itself and that she had forgotten all about this silly notion of hers. I was, in fact, gratified to have our old life returned to us and I found I could appreciate it anew.

Isabelle had been spared, as no doubt many of her friends had tried to warn her, from making what surely would have been a horrendous mistake.

Now it wasn't a mistake she was making.

No, while I enjoyed the unparalleled beauty of the bleak skies, reveling in the stormy sea-tossed ferry ride to Dublin and, once we had arrived, in the seedy pub culture and haunted seascapes of the Dingle, what Isabelle was making were, quite simply, other plans.

But like a fool, I'd been stupidly elated.

Like a man whose death sentence is, at the last moment, commuted, I felt open and free and reconciled to the world. Never for a moment did I imagine that the government that had condemned and released me might re-arrest me at its whim. I had no way of knowing, of course, what Isabelle was concealing from me during those three weeks of our trip. Perhaps I was naïve, but upon our return home, I was genuinely dismayed to discover that what, for me, had been a full commutation of a capital sentence had been, for her, only its necessary postponement.

She lost no time but immediately began ordering flowers and buying a veil, hiring a clergyman and declaring as her wedding gown the simple white cotton shift that, in a rush of renewed affection, I had purchased for her in a charming little shop in Bath.

I watched, seemingly crippled and mute and incapable of protest, as though from my prison cell to which I had been summarily returned, too dazed to even plan an escape, as a Saturday was chosen, a cake ordered and the rose garden on the Pacific Palisades designated as the perfect spot.

"What do you mean? You don't want these, then?" our florist asked me, arranging the halo of flowers Isabelle wished to wear, as a garland, around her veil, when I finally found my voice and said, "I can't go through with it—isn't it obvious, Isabelle?—and I'm telling you now before things get too far out of hand."

"Too far out of hand, Charles?" she said. "Too far out of hand?"

"Too far out of hand," I said.

"The fucking wedding is tomorrow morning!" she screamed. "I think we can safely say that things have gotten too far out of hand!"

"Well, I understand why you might think that," I said, as soothingly as I could before she cut me off.

"Ooh, this is just like him!" she confided to the florist, bitterly rehearsing for her, a perfect stranger, the extensive, intimate and—yes, I will be the first to admit it—neurotic details of our lives together, while I sat on a high stool, surrounded by sprigs of baby's breath, nodding my head in agreement and feeling like a cad, not only towards Isabelle, whose heart I understood I was again and perhaps irrevocably breaking, but also towards this florist, a local woman, against whom I had no complaint and whose small shop, because it was in the middle of our neighborhood, I would have to pass every day, reminding her every day of how I, a typical male epithalamiophobe, had forced her to sacrifice her work for me.

It never occurred to me to simply pay her for her flowers, and offer her a tip. No, instead, I listened and nodded, empathizing, in spite of myself, with the two of them as they, like sisters, commiserated about this problematic fellow and the male race whose representative he was, this exasperating half-man, this Charles Belski, whose form and function I had been forced to assume like an actor who, though he auditioned for the heroic lead, is given instead the part of a minor comic drudge.

(At times, it's true, I *do* feel as though I were playing Shakespeare's Bottom in *A Midsummer Night's Dream,* forced to perform the majority of my role while suffocating inside the head of an ass!)

And yet, despite what should have been, at this point, her very real doubts concerning my suitability as a husband—or perhaps nervous that these doubts might prevent her from attaining that long-sought goal—Isabelle forged willfully ahead, so that the next day I found myself in a suit and tie, standing beneath a tree, wind-whipped on the Pacific Palisades, surrounded (as though by a lynch mob) by a small circle of our friends, mostly women of Isabelle's acquaintance, one of whom was reading, at Isabelle's request, Wallace Stevens' "Final Soliloquy of the Interior Paramour," while below us the agate-green sea pounded the yellow beaches and the Ferris wheel and the merry-go-round on the Santa Monica Pier turned like giant cogs in an enormous machine.

Morning joggers ran past us on either side, a few of them stopping, like tourists, to gawk, as the Unitarian minister, whom Isabelle had instructed *under no circumstances!* to mention the name of Christ, pointed his finger, accusingly, at my chest and, staring me in the eye, as though with daggers drawn, dared me to repeat the vows he himself had no apparent fear of uttering, after which there was, as I recall, a brief kiss and a smattering of applause, as though one of the three of us had performed some remarkable or laudable task.

a complicated gesture of displeasure

And now we trudge across the road to our room, the blinking
lights from the motel sign reflected in the many puddles we have
to jump across to reach it.

Dinner was a miserable affair. Our food, arriving on large,
steamless platters, looked as though it had been prepared weeks
ago, the rice noodles braided in thick clumps, the corn glazed
in a gelid sauce, the peas hard and only partially unfrozen. The
shrimp, rubbery and not quite pink, resembled human ears that
had fallen (perhaps from the old cooks' heads) right into the
boiling pot.

Through the kitchen door, open on its hinge, I could see the two of them shouting at each other, their harsh Mandarin a thick gargle of throaty diphthongs.

The place was so sickening I could barely bring myself to stay and did so only for Isabelle's sake. She was completely drained, having driven through the storms, and although she was hungry (*famished* was the word she used), I was anything but, feeling weak and fluish from the rain and the long day's ordeal.

Speaking low, so the waiter would not hear, I insisted we order from the regular menu, eschewing the overpriced specials and silencing Isabelle's protests with a cutting glare. After all, why pay more for food that you know in advance will be no good?

"I don't suppose there's any point in sending it back," Isabelle said, miserable at the sight of the revolting farrago the waiter eventually placed before us. Still, in a complicated gesture of displeasure, I insisted upon eating it.

And now, rain-imprisoned inside our motel room, with the meal souring in my mouth, I sit upon the bed and sip at the plum wine we've taken, I presume illegally, from the restaurant, running my grease-sheathed tongue across my grease-shielded palette.

Outside, the wind howls like the chorus in Mahler's *Symphony of a Thousand*. Something wooden knocks arrhythmically against something metal.

I kick my shoes off and remove my wet socks and pull back

the covers on the bed, only to discover tawny cigarette burns stippled here and there across its stiff sheets.

"Four dollars. Four fucking dollars, Belski, and we could have had the specials!"

Isabelle leans against the bathroom door, wringing out her hair, her face bland and pinched from hunger. Glaring like a basilisk, she crosses her arms, creating a momentary shelf for her breasts.

Although she possesses many notable and even noble qualities, the ability to remain simultaneously hungry and rational is not one of them.

In fact, she is now so transformed by her anger that I barely recognize her — an experience not unlike what I imagine the faculty in religion at the University of Chicago must have gone through when rumors of Mircea Eliade's youthful involvement with the Iron Guard began to surface. By that I mean: you live with someone, you work with her, you imagine you know her completely, only to discover that you've in fact married a Romanian fascist.

"Oh, fuck you, Charles. You're the Romanian fascist!"

(Perhaps I have extended the metaphor too far.)

"You're the one who's tyrannizing me with this fucking agreement!"

"I should have known," I say.

"An agreement which no one in his right mind would ever expect his wife to live up to."

"Nevertheless," I say.

"No, there is no nevertheless, Charles."

"Nevertheless," I say.

"No, I'm voiding the agreement," she says.

"You can't void the agreement, Isabelle."

"Fuck the agreement!"

"The agreement can't be fucked."

"No, it can be fucked! As of this moment, the agreement is null and void, Charles." And she pronounces the single syllable of my name as though she were some spoiled child's bitter and unmarried nanny. "Oooh, I'm just so sick of having to push you into everything. I have to push and push you into everything, you resist and you resist, you're miserable and you make me miserable, and then after I'm miserable, then and only then do you start to enjoy yourself!"

Her cheeks turn crimson, her eyes blaze like the rings of an alchemical fire, her nostrils flare out in delicate wings. She cocks her elbows at forty-five degrees, her thumbs tucked inside her fists, and I have to admit that she's quite attractive when she becomes impassioned. In fact, it's all I can do not to throw her onto the bed and end our argument by ravishing her beneath the uncomprehending eyes of the moose head hanging above us.

Before I can act, however, my stomach, filled to the brim with execrable Chinese food, knots in a reflex of panic.

What if she's right? I can't help thinking. What if it's true that she's had to push me into everything, forcing me to travel, for instance, when I have no wish to travel, forcing me to marry when I had no wish to marry, attempting to force children onto me now when I have no wish for children? And the truth is, none of it has been in any way transforming. I'm still the Charles Belski I've always been: bristling, hypersensitive, critical and prone to gloomy reverie. Is it even possible to change? I have to wonder. Is it even possible to die to oneself, so to speak, to strip away one's history, one's identity, one's education, one's cultural or ethnic indoctrination, and emerge, as though from a grave, resurrected and transformed?

Or do we all merely end up like Albert and Gladys, lugging all our old furniture into our underground cottage so that our new life beneath the earth is no different from the one we lived upon it?

Sick at heart, I cover my head with the blankets and curl up in a fetal position, keeping an eye on Isabelle through a little crack I leave in the covers. We're long-schooled in this dark pleasure of whipping one another into an emotional fracas and I imagine that she will rip the covers from me, exposing me to the glare of the overhead lights, tearing into me with a renewed vigor, as though I were her prisoner in an interrogation cell. However, she leaves me alone, and I end up feeling ridiculous and small, lying here like a man in a Thurber cartoon, hiding from his wife in their bed.

As a further and final provocation, I pretend to fall asleep, breathing softly through my mouth and emphasizing a small catch at the base of my throat, but Isabelle ignores this completely.

From beneath the blankets, I hear the muffled sound of a woman's voice behind a wall call out, "Edgar, what?" and then a thousand creaking noises seem to overwhelm my senses. Perhaps it's the heat beneath the stuffy covers or the effects of the alcohol or simply the weariness I'm feeling, but soon I am no longer pretending and am actually asleep, a regrettable lapse on my part, as I will realize only later, when I've awoken and, squinting myopically in the darkened room, discover Isabelle moving about on top of me.

Too distraught to sleep, as she will explain to me the following morning, she removed her contact lenses and sipped her plum wine while flipping through the television stations, their spinning images reflecting inside the curved lenses of her glasses. Sitting crosslegged on the bed, she flossed her teeth and watched a free promo for a porn movie. She rolled the used thread of floss up like a miniature electrical cord and threw it into the wastebasket. She took her temperature with the basal thermometer she carries everywhere with her these days. She brushed her teeth and climbed out of her clothes and gazed down at my shapeless form. Pulling back the covers and allowing me to breathe, she stood over me. She watched me, she says, as though she were the Minotaur watching that sleeping girl in one of those pen-and-ink sketches by Picasso—or by Hockney after Picasso, she couldn't remember which—her heart torn equally by rage and pity; rage, because how dare I humiliate her by sleeping through an argument as important as this; pity, because, at the sight of me breathing through my mouth like a little boy who can't defend himself, she brimmed with a maternal longing that somehow blurred into a highly eroticized desire. She told herself that, of course, when I said I didn't want children, I couldn't possibly mean it. Certainly, I hadn't thought the issue through.

Returning to the bathroom, she showered off the day's grime, the rain and the red clay, and watched it all spiraling down the rust-rimmed drain.

Drying herself, she entered the room. The lights from the motel's sign, blinking through the drapes' loose mesh, illuminated the wall above the bed in alternating bursts of blue and red. She slipped off the white towel and climbed upon the easily arousible staff of her drowsing husband. And taking it into herself, rocking backwards and forwards, she raised the covers like a flag across her back.

as round and circular as a bowl of fruit

Isabelle's body grows as round and as circular as a bowl of fruit. She's fully pregnant and her breasts are swollen, their areolae have darkened and empurpled like morning glories, and a plum-colored seam has appeared on her bowed abdomen, running from her sternum past her navel to her pubis. Her hair has thickened, and her fingers. She can no longer wear her wedding ring and keeps it dangling instead on a chain hanging between her exaggerated breasts.

She laughs easily these days, more easily than I've ever known her to, throwing back her head and clapping her hands; and she eats voraciously, wolfing down great quantities of food, especially blueberries. I can't bring her enough of them. They're no longer in season, but she doesn't care if they're expensive, only that they're ripe, and her teeth and lips are habitually stained an iridescent blue.

I've never found her more alluring, although the sight of her can be enervating. All that new life swimming around inside the fluids of her ever-expanding body is exhausting to contemplate, and very often I have to lie down in her presence.

She stands before the mirror, her hair in one hand, swiveling this way and that, admiring the reflection of her girth, marveling at it, in fact, as I am, lying on our futon on the floor. She never used to wear a bra, but now, unaccustomed to the burdens of her bosom, she cannot afford not to, although she loathes the awful things and often pulls a cotton halter on instead.

Slipping on a rose-colored T-shirt, she raises her arms over her head, her elbows laddering one above the other. Her head appears through the hole, and she frees the hanks of her hair with two swift karate-like chops on either side of her neck. She steps into an oversized pair of coveralls, the only thing these days that can contain her blossoming circumferences.

Unpregnant women all look like scarecrows to me now, lifeless stick figures, and it's all I can do not to grab Isabelle and undress her immediately. The thrill of unclasping her coveralls and unbuttoning their brass buttons is an experience as sensual as Salome's Dance of the Seven Veils, and soon, like John the Baptist, we have both lost our heads, and she is on her hands and knees on the futon in the only position left to us, her belly hanging inches above the mattress.

I pull her near me, although both of us know this can't go on much longer. The baby must be *right there!* by now.

Because she works four mornings a week, baking pastries in an all-natural café, her hair is fragrant with honey, cinnamon, cardamom, and our bedsheets are gritty with flour. When she leaves this morning, she's slightly disheveled, her cheeks in a high ruby blush. I imagine her arriving as the bread bakers put in their final hour, moving wordlessly inside the silence that comes at the end of an all-night shift. The hair on their arms white with flour, their heads beneath snowy bandanas, they've long run out of conversation and communicate, not even with gestures, but through unarticulated intention.

Even the radio, which blared through the night, seems muted and reserved, as Rosenthal, the head baker, in violation of all health and safety codes, sticks his paw into the mixing tub to check the dough's consistency. His assistant, O'Malley, glazed-eyed, with two wings of raven hair in braids between thin shoulders, scrapes the cantles from the kneading table before slathering its surfaces with oil.

Isabelle loves this time, before sunrise, when it's quiet, and the air is cool and blue. The smell of newly baked bread is every-where. Happily, she pours herself a cup of coffee and opens the front door, leaving the screen door latched. Holding the mug in one hand, she kneels to rummage through a basket on the floor, its wide mouth brimming with day-old bread, fishing from its depths a loaf aquamarine with mold.

The refrigerator cases hum wetly, their shelves stocked with cartons of wheatgrass juice, cans of all-natural soda, tall bottles of rice milk.

With her belly on her lap, Isabelle sits on a high stool at the breakfast counter, sipping her coffee and planning her morning's baking: Ischler torteletes, chocolate biscotti, perhaps a large hazelnut torte.

Dreaming of her caffeine-scented kisses, I lie in bed, listening to *Das Lied von der Erde* on our CD-clock-radio.

"*Ich suche Ruhe für mein einsam Herz. / Ich wandle nach der Heimat, meiner Stätte,*" the mezzosoprano sings in the song cycle's concluding lullaby. "I seek rest for my lonely heart. / I journey to my homeland, to my resting place."

It's a curious fact, but in an embryo, the heart forms as a single pulsating organ, gradually separating into its articulated chambers as the fetus grows, its two halves partitioned permanently only at the moment of birth, when the lungs begin to function and the hole between the halves, the ductus arteriosum, closes. It's a violent moment for the fetus. The umbilical cord is clamped or severed, the placenta is torn away, and the child's heart, as though broken in two, is now forever divided against itself.

"Ewig . . . Ewig . . . ," the mezzosoprano whispers the final words of the final song, "eternally . . . eternally . . . ," and with my arms behind my head, I stare at the ceiling, thinking about our unborn child, nestled beneath Isabelle's bosom, its small heart beating, innocent of its own inevitable breaking.

kindertotenlieder or,
day care among the paste-eaters

Something about small children tends to make me sad.

I can barely drop Franny off at her day care without coming away from it mildly depressed. It has something to do, I think, with seeing them, these children, sitting in their little knee-dimpling circles, their little hands manipulating their little tools: their miniature scissors, their cigar-fat markers, their squat jars of clumpy paste—the kind unhappy children used to eat (at least they did when I was little), running the paste-clotted stick, like a Thai hors d'oeuvre, across their bumpy tongues.

Isabelle loses all patience with me when I speak of it, but we tend to treat our children as though we were preparing them for a life in an Aborigine village, with songs and papercrafts, little circle dances, and storytellers arriving on odd schedules. We allow and even encourage them to mark up their bodies, their faces, their hands, with free and colorful designs.

It's no wonder so many of them will fail in later life.

And Franny must feel the same way I do, because I have to struggle with her each day I drive her in, forcing her from my arms and into the little play group. She clings to my neck, strangling me on the days I wear a tie, screaming, "Daddy, Daddy, please, not yet!"

With her thick glasses and the little blank diary she carries, in lieu of a blanket, for reassurance, she resembles a nervous, a reluctant, anthropologist, afraid to have to fend for herself on this strange island of wild and happy primitives: Glue-Eaters' Island! I can't help shuddering, even thinking of it. And it's my own fault, really. I allow her to sleep in. Neither Isabelle nor I have the heart to rouse her so early from her bed, as though she were a milkman! She's only three, after all, and this way I can get a little work done before she wakes up and begins issuing her tiny, frazzling demands, standing in her crib like Mussolini on the balustrade.

(Who knew such a small child could be so imperious, so shrill?)

And invariably we are the last ones to arrive at her day care because of it, arriving literally hours after the tiny group has formally cohered, so that Franny's entry into it each day is uncertain, causing her, each day, to cling to my neck and scream. Her caregivers, summoned by this shrieking, approach us from all sides. Smiling knowingly, indulgently, not unsympathetically, they attempt to sever her from my arms.

"No!—Daddy!—please!" Franny yowls or screams or rather in actual fact whispers. She whispers this plea, albeit shrilly and directly into my ear, her small teeth pressed hard against it, her forehead banging wildly into my temple; wanting above all not to be embarrassed, she whispers in an attempt to remind me privately of the bond we share, a blood tie that by rights must supercede the desires of these grasping others with their paltry claims to a pallid civic authority.

And what can I do, torn as I am between an instinctual need to protect her and a very real desire to immediately surrender her up to them? After all, I have oceans of work yet to swim through this morning. Long since promised to its publishers, my monograph on Mahler's *Kindertotenlieder* remains hopelessly unfinished, my notes and drafts gnawing at me, like a rat trapped in my briefcase, suffocating for want of air.

I do nothing, nothing. Or little. Very little.

I smile back at them, these smiling teachers, the harried, embarrassed father, self-humiliating and ineffectual, clichés clinging to me like mussels to a pier, while Franny, oblivious to our adult complicities, continues to struggle between us, locked as if in a death grip, kicking and clawing, pinching at my shirt, trying to save herself. And from what?

From what?

From a carefree day of play with this merry, mucusy band of rascals, these parasitic blobs of protoplasm, these refugees from Glue-Eaters' Island!

I can barely think of them without growing despondent, the penitential prayers my fellow Jews and I send up to Heaven every year on the Day of Atonement ringing like a death knell in my ear: *Who by water? Who by fire? Who because he wore glasses or glanced at his nails like a girl? Who because, laughing, she slobbered milk through her nose?*

(It's their innocence, I realize, that depresses me most, their small and happy ignorance of their own abysmal fragility.)

Working now as a great gaggle, Franny's teachers are able, finally, to snatch her from my arms. We're adults, after all; we're stronger; we outnumber her and, besides, we're working against her from all sides, with me merely pretending to offer her my aid. Tears stream down her cheeks from behind her boxy black rims. Red-faced, she wails like a heretic being dragged down the corridors of the Inquisitor's Palace. Her little fingers curled, her pudgy arms flailing, she reaches out but is unable to grasp me, her betraying father: whether for assistance or to slap me in the face, I cannot tell.

In the silence that follows her deportation from the room, the remaining teachers turn to me, presenting concerned and considerate faces. Possessing the bland equanimity of government-sponsored torturers, they offer their reassurances.

"She'll stop crying," they say. "She always does."

"Just as soon as you leave."

But I don't wait, not even long enough to wonder if I believe them or to see if what they say is true.

Instead, I make a quick and embarrassed dash past the rat in the aquarium, past the twenty or so noodle-and-yarn-constructed portraits of the smiling sun, out the purple-and-yellow door, into the morning-drenched playground with its tire swings and its climbing ropes and its multileveled wooden platforms, through the thigh-high picket gate, its little tin bell tinkling as a warning against the possible intrusion of kidnappers, pederasts, child pornographers, arriving at my car, where I sit, gripping the steering wheel and staring at my hands, a plastic grin of gratitude plastered to my face, as though I myself had been eating glue and the silly grin had somehow gotten itself stuck there.

WHICH IS WHY Isabelle drives Franny in to day care the following day. It's just as well. Franny is more disciplined around Isabelle, it's true. Isabelle has only to say, "Franny: One! . . . Two! . . ." (she doesn't even have to say "Three!") and Franny snaps to, instantly, a little soldier.

It breaks my heart to see it, this numbers-induced obedience with its concomitant terror arrived at as if by mathematical formulae, when even Isabelle admits she has no idea what she is threatening to do if she ever reaches *three* and Franny has never even thought to inquire into the consequences of arriving there.

And yet, for some reason, *three* is terrifying and black.

(I would imagine it has something to do with Isabelle's Catholic upbringing, with dark-cowled nuns and a punitive misuse of the Holy Trinity, had I not seen it work cross-culturally, on many different children and always with a similar result.)

ACCORDING TO ISABELLE, carrying Franny in is my first mistake. No, not even my first, probably my twenty-first by that hour.

"You have to walk her in beside you, Charles." Which is what Isabelle did this morning. "And then because she's already on her feet, transferring her from my skirt into Suneetha's wasn't such a problem."

Isabelle lifts the lid off the wok and a bouquet of steam blooms, rising from inside it. Bending at the waist, she peers beneath the pot, adjusting the burner's blue flame.

"I simply said, 'Now, Francesca, Mommy is very busy today and she can't stay and have a fight with you, okay?'"

(By referring to herself in the third person and by addressing Franny by her legal name, Isabelle had hoped to impress upon our small daughter the full weight of her remarks, as though she were reading from, or issuing, a legal decree.)

"'When Mommy drops you off, Francesca, she needs you to help her by simply saying good-bye—okay?—and without a fuss.'"

(Here, an explicit request is made, expectations are openly addressed. No longer its unwilling object, the child is made a part-ner to the bargain, called in for her assistance, as though she were a consultant, a specialist, say, in childhood separation-anxiety disorders, which, in many ways, I suppose, she actually is.)

"'Mommy has to get to work early and so you and she have to have a quick good-bye, okay?'"

"''Kay, Mommy,'" Franny is reported to have said, and pleas-antly enough, sucking on her thumb in the car seat in back, clutching her little diary against the side of her chest with her el-bow, holding on to her ear with the other hand, the black stems of her glasses raised slightly and tilted, the frames falling crookedly across her face.

Isabelle tosses a quarter cup of curry into the wok and our kitchen fills with its muscular yellow pungency.

Her hair, cut short now, is as spiky as a military cadet's, and she is trim again, her abdomen flat beneath the fabric of her flannel dress. She slides the head of the spatula beneath the rice like a shovel into sand and turns it.

"We exchanged a calm and, I might add, highly rational kiss, Charles." With Franny neither hugging nor clinging nor plead-ing. "In fact, she'd forgotten all about me before I'd even left." Isabelle smacks the neck of the spatula against the metal rim of the wok, dislodging an aggregate of rice. "At that moment, I had no more importance to her than the threshold she had to cross to get into the room."

• • •

LISTENING TO MAHLER'S *Kindertotenlieder* in my office, following along with the score, I can think of little besides the glue-eaters I myself have known, glue-eaters from my own childhood.

It's only now that I realize how unhappy these children must have been.

Teddy Ollinger, whose mother stabbed herself eleven times in the kitchen with a kitchen knife when we were in the fifth grade, was a glue-eater. Also Cherise Skaggs who (or so rumor had it) had sex with her brother Kim in the family attic, three doors down from our house, more or less around the same time.

Teddy used to nibble the plastic stick inserted through the paste jar's circular lid, while Cherise dribbled squiggly white lines of the viscous liquid up and down the arc of her extended tongue, which she'd then retract and undulate, smacking it against the roof of her mouth, her eyes moist with pleasure at the other children's gagging yucks and oohs.

"Do you know what that's made of?" we cried, as it turned out, quite uselessly.

"Horse bones!" we cried.

"You're eating horse bones, Cherise! Or don't you know that?"

But either she didn't know or, knowing, didn't care. She was too hungry, I see now: more for the attention than for the glue.

The music fills my office, the contralto swelling in brightening darkening tones, "... *von keinem Sturm erschrecket, von Gottes Hand bedecket, Sie ruh'n, Sie ruh'n wie in der Mutter Haus, wie in der Mutter Haus,"* its sadness discernible even through the tinny speakers I keep upon my desk.

Kindertotenlieder. Songs of Dead Children.

Mahler began the cycle shortly before the birth of his second daughter. A pregnant Alma, fearing superstitiously for the lives of her children, begged him to abandon the work. Swept up in its creation, Mahler refused to consider her irrational fears, and in 1907, three years after the piece's completion, when their younger daughter Maria died of scarlet fever and diphtheria at the age of only four-and-a-half, Alma couldn't help blaming him, despite his obvious devastation.

The music is somber, stirring, eloquent, although the lyric (by the poet Rückert) is slightly overripe in places, a little sentimental or precious, seemingly suggesting that mourning a death can be a beautiful, an ennobling, thing made even more beautiful or noble when the object of one's grief is an innocent child. In death, it's true, children are, at least, finally quiet. They don't jump with their shoes on the sofas, bullying one another and prattling their nonsensical chatter, getting everything they touch (including the insides of their own mouths!) sticky as they devour their small portions of adhesive substances, although I'm certain that's not what Mahler or Rückert had in mind.

"Enough, Charles! You're terrifying Franny!" Isabelle shrills, dishing out the curried rice from a large ceramic bowl that she holds, by one arm, against her hip.

"No he's not, Mommy. I mean, he is, he is, but just a little . . . just a little bit."

Franny drags a greasy fish stick through the rainpuddle of ketchup she's daubed onto her plate. She's outgrown her high-chair and refuses to use a booster, and must stand on the chair to reach, balancing with one hand against the tabletop as she manipulates her food with the other, her diary, that inexplicable source of comfort, lying opened beside her on the table.

Generally, I can't stomach ketchup. The smell and even the sight of it make me queasy, as do the other major American condiments, mustard and mayonnaise. I have no idea from where this sense of delicacy derives, but it seems to have something to do with the viscosity of these foods, and tonight, it's even worse. The ketchup, gathered in its typical half-dry-half-moist residue along the rings of the bottle's corkscrew neck, reminds me of glue and of glue-eating and I find that I can't help thinking of Cherise Skaggs in various positions in her family's attic with her brother Kim, a notorious bully who terrorized our neighbor-hood, and who once killed a cat with his bare hands before burying it at the side of their house and who forced me once, on my hands and knees, to eat grass from my own lawn during a late-afternoon kickball game, the members of both teams looking on helplessly from all sides as the setting sun drained its light from the sky.

"He *killed* it?" Franny's eyes are even more enormous than they normally are simply magnified by her thick lenses.

"He said it'd been hit by a car, Franny. It was shivering and scraggly."

"He probably thought he was putting it out of its misery," Isabelle says.

"But was he, Daddy? Was he putting it out of its misery?"

"I don't think so, Franny."

"Charles . . ."

"That wasn't very nice of him, was it, Daddy?"

"No, Franny, it wasn't."

"He could have taken it to the doctor's."

"He could have," I agree.

"But some children come from unhappy homes, Franny," Isabelle explains, "and so they do bad things."

"But was he bad, Daddy? He was bad, wasn't he?" Franny says, looking, in her pink overalls and her boxy rectangular frames, like a miniature Shostakovich visiting a workers' agricultural collective in the Ukraine.

"Very bad, Franny."

Isabelle scolds us both: "I don't think Franny needs to be hearing this, Charles."

"It's okay, Mommy, I'm old enough. What else did he do, Daddy?"

"Well, Franny, for one thing, the whole Skaggs family claimed that they could ride their bicycles on our driveway because our driveway wasn't concrete like the other driveways on our street."

"It wasn't, Daddy?"

"No, it was paved, you see, and covered in tar, *like* the street, and so they said it *was* the street and that they could ride their bicycles on it anytime they wished."

"But could they?" she asks.

"*No, of course not!* It was still private property!" I say, and the oddly emotional note, trembling in my voice, surprises even me.

"Oh, for God's sake, Charles. How long are you going to grieve over this?" Isabelle asks with a degree of (I suppose) justifiable exasperation.

The Skaggs house was only three doors down from ours, and my sisters and I were forced to carpool to school with them. Both Juanita and Elwin had children from previous marriages, Cherise being, I believe, their only child in common. (So perhaps it was only half-incest, if incest at all, when she and Kim had sex in the attic. If indeed they did. I have no idea, actually. I merely heard these rumors then and repeat them now, unverified, although, I have to say, it wouldn't surprise me because the entire family was strange.) The children, for example, were allowed to drink sodas for breakfast and this seemed as exotic to me as Elwin's silver flat-top and the red bowties he customarily wore.

It was also quite strange meeting Kim in his own house after having been terrorized by him in the street. In front of his parents, he was an entirely different person. It was as though the scorched earth policy he conducted outside the house belonged to an entirely different life, and every morning, we seemed to suffer from a form of collective amnesia, all of us forgetting who Kim really was and what he had done to us, so that we could, instead, exchange pleasant good mornings with his stepmother Juanita, who, to my profound confusion, and despite her jet-black bouffant with its Spanish side curls, appeared not to have a single ounce of Hispanic blood in her veins.

Every morning, she fried their toast and bacon, and the children tippled from their green bottles of Coca-Cola the last energizing sips of the day. It was all I could do to breathe in their kitchen with Kim slouched over his breakfast, his greasy hair parted on one side, his heavy black hornrims sliding down the bridge of his nose, his cheeks and chin aggravated by the red pustules of his acne. Lingering over his food like a strange animal that is savage, but only when encountered in the bush, never in its own lair, he taunted me silently, smirking as though at a joke only he and I understood.

"You know, Charles," Isabelle says flatly, "the only reason people find children's cruelty so disturbing is that, unlike adults, children are cruel without having an ideology."

"What's an ideology?" Franny says.

But of course, I know perfectly well what Isabelle means. I've heard her often enough on the subject. Roughly paraphrased, her argument precedes along these lines: In submission to various ideologies, adults build gas chambers in Europe and drop bombs on civilian Japan and slaughter millions in Cambodia and rape scores of women in Bosnia and starve them to death in

Ethiopia, all the while effecting coups against popularly elected governments in Chile and El Salvador, destroying the natural resources of the rain forests, and wiping out species at a rate of one a day, so that anybody who manages to survive this industrialized reign of terror and greed will have only a fragment of a tattered planet left to live on, and you're upset because *for no reason at all!* the neighborhood bully rode his bicycle on your driveway without asking your family's permission?

"Could *somebody* please move that disgusting bottle of ketchup off the table!" I say, but no one listens to me and I have to pick it up myself with my napkin, holding my breath and moving it away.

"Well, was anybody ever mean to you, Mommy?" Franny asks, sucking her thumb.

"To me?" Isabelle says, as though startled by the idea.

"When you were my age"— Franny removes her thumb from her mouth —"was anybody ever mean to you?"

"No, no . . . well . . ." Isabelle's face darkens. "I mean, I don't think so . . ." she says, and she sighs and her chest deflates and her shoulders drop and for a moment she simply stares at the grain of wood in the table, rubbing it absently with her thumb.

"Well. Once, I guess . . . there *was* this girl named Janie McCoy. This was in the sixth grade and she was new to our school and we became friends very quickly, Franny, much too quickly, as a matter of fact. We spent almost every afternoon together at first."

"Doing what, Mommy?"

"Doing what? Well, you know, just silly things."

"Like what, Mommy?"

"Like what? Well. For instance: once, I remember, we ate ice cream in the shower."

"In the shower!"

"Was it on?"

"No, of course not, Charles."

"And you weren't undressed or anything?"

"Of course not!"

"And then what happened?" Franny says.

"And then what happened, Franny? And then, well, I guess, the groovy-doovy kids asked Janie to be their friend and they told her she couldn't be their friend unless she stopped being mine."

"Well, no wonder if you used words like *groovy-doovy*," I say.

"Oh, for God's sake, Charles, just shut up!" Isabelle says, looking immediately and repentantly at Franny, who has brought her little hands to her mouth, shocked by the use of this forbidden phrase.

"Anyway, I mean, she wasn't even that cool, you know, but one day, she just told me she couldn't be my friend anymore." Isabelle looks helplessly at me. "Isn't that horrible?"

BECAUSE ISABELLE IS too depressed over Janie McCoy to do it, I put Franny to bed, placing her feetfirst into her crib. Immediately, she begins jumping up and down inside it, the mattress springs squeaking and wheezing and the little plastic beads inside her Playskool mirror rattling like a crazed maracaist.

"Stop it, Franny!" I say, wearied by this extravagant display of pointless enthusiasm, but my words only make her legs pump harder. She raises her knees to her chest, the nubbed feet of her Dr. Denton's supplying all the traction she needs.

"I've asked you to stop nicely now," I say, as she turns her back on me, jumping even more frenetically, gripping the railing with one diminutive hand, allowing the other to wave free, as though she were dancing a Charleston, oblivious to my commands, so that I have no choice but to shout, "Franny. One! . . . Two! . . ."

And to my amazement, she drops to her knees, panicking and scurrying for cover.

"Okay, okay, o-*kaaay!*" she says pleadingly.

It's as though a bomb had gone off near a marionette factory and all her strings have snapped.

I raise the covers quickly, before she can reverse herself, and straighten them out, folding a triangular flap over her in one enormous arc: comforter-blanket-sheet rolling over her like a giant tsunami. She scrunches up beneath them, a drowner resisting their warmth and their weight, and I can't help thinking: If numbers are so frightening to her, what possible chance does she stand against less abstract concepts? Nouns, for instance: people, places, things. These are what should properly be terrifying her, not numbers! And yet, so far, I've been incapable of inculcating any kind of self-protective fear into her. She still smiles and waves brightly at strangers, sending out her cheerful greetings indiscriminately, even to the most dangerous-looking hoodlums lurking in our neighborhood, shouting up at me, loudly enough for all to hear, "But, Daddy, why are you crossing the street? I want to say hello to my friends," whenever I turn her stroller self-defensively away.

("Because the Number Three is slouching against the wall of that liquor store, Franny, that's why!" I'll say the next time the situation recurs, although now that I have the perfect reply, of course it never will.)

She gathers herself into a tighter ball and rolls beneath the blankets until the corners are untucked and her legs exposed.

"I can't sleep. I'm too wiggly," she complains.

"Try," I say.

Her clunky glasses — for some reason, she'd insisted on getting the ugliest frames available — are on the nightstand next to a plastic cup of water and her diary, and she squints at me without them, holding up a tiny, insistent finger.

"One song Daddy one song one song Daddy just one song Daddy one song Daddy please!"

She's a bit of an insomniac, I'm afraid. Even as an infant, she struggled against sleep, her eyes blackening with half-moons, the wheel of her mind unable to stop itself. Waiting for her to drop off at the end of the day can be a tedious experience for everyone involved, and with Isabelle driving her in in the mornings, she no longer has the luxury of sleeping late.

It never worked because Franny only forced herself to stay awake to hear the songs through to their ends, requesting one and then another of her favorites, but it was Isabelle's idea to sing her to sleep in the hope that music would somehow force her into becoming drowsy.

Isabelle is not much of a singer; nor does she come from an overly musical family, but for reasons that remain obscure to me, she chose "Goodnight, Irene" as her principal bedtime tune. A relic from her own childhood, a treasure she wished to pass on to her daughter, the song was so familiar to her that she had never actually heard it. This is not an uncommon experience. In fact, it wasn't until almost a year later, with the words tumbling out of her mouth like malevolent acrobats, that Isabelle realized that this creaky old lament, this quaint hillbilly yodel, the droning choruses of which she'd been crooning faithfully into our daughter's tender and unformed psyche, was nothing less than a sentimental suicide note, its themes concerned principally with madness, depression, infidelity, pedophilia, suicide, drug addiction, compulsive gambling, drunkenness, and homicide.

(I refer you to the lyric, if you don't believe me.)

Unable to sustain his jealous hatred for his child-bride Irene, the song's narrator finally confesses his love for her after either murdering her or attempting to. It isn't clear, but what *is* clear is that the narrator loves Irene, God knows he does, he will, and he always will, at least until the seas run dry: "If Irene turns her back on me, I'm gonna take morphine and die."

It was this line, I believe, that alerted Isabelle finally to the song's darker themes. She felt terrible, of course, distraught that she had somehow poisoned our daughter's weltanschauung at its root.

How could she have never heard the lyric before?

"I just didn't, Charles. Now leave me alone. Okay!"

Imagine singing a song like that every night of her life to a ten-month-old baby!

"Shut up! Just shut up, okay? I feel bad enough as it is!"

Worse: by this time, Franny had grown attached to the melody and refused to hear anything else before falling asleep.

So, undaunted (although guiltily), desperate for a solution and with no other choice, Isabelle revised the lyric, turning its heart-embittered stanzas into a nice little ditty about magical space travel:

> *Last Saturday night, I met Franny,*
> *a girl most honest and true,*
> *I said I'd take her on a trip.*
> *We're gonna travel to the moon.*

Franny and I went to the moon,
the night was wondrous and bright.
We met a lady living there
who was filled with wonder and light.

The lady was a magic queen.
She sprinkled us with stardust.
She said to rest our weary eyes,
To sleep and to give her our trust.

Goodnight, Franny-y-y.
Goodnight, Franny.
Goodnight, Franny; goodnight, Franny.
I'll see you in my dreams.

It's this song that I sing to Franny tonight.

We sing it together, actually; she in a light, quavering line; I, deeper and almost in a whisper, waiting for her to drop out of our duo, but of course, she never does. At the end of it, she's still awake, staring at the ceiling like a traveling salesman in a cheap motel fretting about the day's paltry sales.

I bend down to give her a kiss, pulling back the tangled mesh of her black hair. Her breath reeks of the stale scent of sucked thumb. Mobiles dangle above her, turning in their gyres. Her face is serious and concerned.

"Daddy," she says, squinting up at me.

"What is it now, Franny?" I say.

"There's just one thing I don't understand."

It's evident she's given the matter a great deal of thought.

"If you don't sing them to your children," she says, "then what are songs *for*?"

"What are songs for?" I say.

"Yeah, if you don't sing them to your children."

I admit I'm unprepared for the question and I ramble on unconvincingly, or so it seems to me, about beauty, self-expression, commemoration, celebration, and the blues.

I recall that Teddy Ollinger sang "One Tin Soldier" once in front of our entire sixth-grade class. I can't now recall the occasion, a talent show or a music report of some kind. It may even have been earlier, in the fourth or fifth grade.

Teddy wore two bright pink snowballs of rouge on his cheeks and a tall, furry Nutcracker-style hat with three yellow circles running up it vertically. The yellow circles and the pink snowballs, a motif, were exactly the same size. (Did he say that his sisters had helped him with the costume or am I only now imagining it?)

He had memorized the song, but not securely, and he had to stare at a fixed point in the back of the room, near where the ceiling joined the wall, concentrating furiously as though the words were written there, while droning them out in a kind of hypnotized trance. He wore colorful suspenders, three inches wide, in style at the time, and his performance, I remember thinking even then, was atrocious, absolute kitsch.

(What I had missed, I realize now, was the overall sadness of the thing.)

Still, his performance went over fairly well—better in fact than anything I'd ever presented to the class, my (I'm certain) tedious reports on the lives of Schubert and Brahms—the class responding to Teddy's comatose, dirgelike singing style with a round of sturdy applause, although this may have been after his mother stabbed herself with a kitchen knife, so that I'm not certain it wasn't out of sympathy.

thousands of now confused druids

As a child, I possessed a highly articulated sense of the romantic.

By six, I was a miniature Dante, searching every face he encountered for a glimpse of his Beatrice, whose likeness I found
in none of the three girls in my Sunday school class, two of whom
were instantly unacceptable to me: Bridget Yorami because she
was overweight and something of a bully, or if not a bully, then
a vulgarian who taught me to pull back my index and third fingers and to hold them behind my raised middle finger with my
thumb, instructions I had not solicited and whose purposes I did
not fully comprehend, as we stood outside our synagogue one
cool Yom Kippur evening.

Leanne Dorfman was not much better. As a result of an intraocular retinoblastoma, she had lost an eye the summer before and now wore a pink eye patch. "Like Moshe Dayan," she said, hopefully, making the best of it, I suppose, but only further compounding my sexual confusions.

(Before I proceed, allow me to say here, should either Leanne or Bridget chance upon these pages, that I cringe at having to mention these ungracious details and do so apologetically, suspecting that they are neither objectively recalled nor justly rendered, and certainly, they reflect poorly only upon myself as a child and not upon these young girls who, though I have kept up with neither of them, are by now, I feel certain, attractive and self-possessed women of early middle age.)

At the time, however, I took their limited appeal as a categorical defeat.

The Jewish community of Karkel, Texas, was small. I was, in fact, the only boy in my Sunday school class, but I understood from things my sisters had told me that, despite this, I was obligated to marry a Jew.

Why I never at the time considered venturing beyond my own grade level, to say nothing of the city limits, in my search for a suitable spouse, is something I can't explain. Perhaps because I was in the first grade, my frame of reference was necessarily limited.

In any case, this left only Lizzie Blumgarten, a skinny girl with two eyes and good manners but little else to recommend her.

We were friends and classmates, Lizzie and I, but even at age six, I understood that there was no erotic spark between us. And yet, in an effort to conform to tribal norms, I asked her out on what in retrospect can be described as my first date, although at the time I hardly thought of it as such.

I retain a small snapshot of the seminal event. In it, we are diminutive stick figures, Lizzie and I, looking down at my dog, Hunter, a cairn terrier, on the occasion of his graduation from obedience school where, over the course of his rigorous training, he had learned apparently nothing. The ceremony was an embarrassing farce, with Hunter refusing to perform any of the tricks asked of him, including the simple task of jumping off a small tub-like platform with a miniature mortar board fastened to his head by an elastic string.

Exasperated, her red hair coming unhinged, the woman who ran the school finally forced him off the overturned tub, sticking a rolled-up diploma into his mouth and inaugurating the applause herself, which was tepid, to say the least.

(Hunter and I were to prove not dissimilar, not only in terms of my own sentimental education, but in regard to my religious training as well, those two paltry hours of Sunday school every week from the time I was six until I was twelve when, coerced into attending an extra hour twice a week in preparation for my bar mitzvah, I allowed Rabbi Kleinblatt to drill into my not infertile brain the simple skill set of recognizing and pronouncing the twenty-two consonants and five vowel markings of the

Hebrew alphabet. He concentrated exclusively on this task while consigning to silence five thousand years of law, history, ritual, philosophy, philology, theology, literature and ethics, to say nothing of grammar, syntax and meaning. Apparently, the simple ability to decipher phonemes was all the elders of our community, in consultation with the good rabbi, deemed necessary for their children's encounter with the Creator of the Universe, who, according to His own account—which none of us had bothered to read—was quite finicky about an inordinate number of things.)

Is it any wonder I married out?

A gentle lad, embarking for the first time into the world from his mother's embrace, I'd run out of marriageable Jewesses.

And yet, this a fortiori conclusion on my part—that because there were no alluring girls in my first-grade Sunday school class, there must therefore be no alluring Jewish women anywhere in the world—was only one of several misunderstandings aggravating an already tortuous childhood.

In public school, for instance, when our principal Mrs. Hèlas became ill and my first-grade teacher Mrs. Appleton asked each of us to make her a get-well card, I folded a piece of construction paper in two and, using a black Crayola, drew a small portrait of Mrs. H. in profile on the front.

It was a simple enough task and she was easy enough to draw, with her grey hair pulled back on her head in a tight bun and her nose jutting forth from her face like half a parallelogram.

I wrote "I HOPE YOUR FEELING BETTER" on the inside of the card and promptly brought it up to Mrs. Appleton at her desk. She glanced at it through those strange glasses she wore, black rims above the lenses and silver hoops beneath, glasses that I associated then and continue to associate, for some reason, with farm folk and that, I see now, aged her severely. She was a grandmotherly figure to me, sexless and benevolent, although at the time she was probably no older than forty-five.

"Very good, Charles, very good," she said. "The only thing, here, is that you may use this word *your* only, like, once in your life."

"Only once in your life?" I said. "I've never heard that before."

"It's confusing, isn't it?" she agreed.

And, indeed, this was startling news.

Never before had anyone — neither my parents nor my sisters, nor my kindergarten teachers, for that matter — mentioned that there were limits to the number of times you could use an individual word.

Surely the rule applied, I reasoned as, stunned, I made my way back to my seat, only in written speech. *Your* was a common word. Everyone I knew used it again and again, often more than once in a single sentence. *Charles, breathe through your nose and get your hair off my pillow* was something my sister Mindy, for example, said quite frequently. And although doing so seemed an impossible task (there were neither synonyms nor substitutions nor metonymical feints) I scrupulously avoided its use to such an extent that I can recall sitting at my desk, two years later, writing an in-class essay, needing the word *your* but thinking, as though I were a clerk out of Kafka or Gogol: Surely, they'll examine my old tests and papers and see that I've used it already.

It was only a matter of time, I knew, before they discovered me. After all, had I not sent the principal a card with the word recklessly scrawled across it, which she probably still had somewhere, tucked inside a drawer, as it was really quite a good likeness, or at least I thought so at the time.

Certainly I had misunderstood her, but what could Mrs. Appleton have meant?

The question bedeviled me for a number of years, at least ten, I know, because I was driving when the realization occurred to me that—*of course!*—I had misspelled the word and what Mrs. Appleton meant was not that one could use the word *your* only once in his life, but that *you're*—(with an apostrophe and an E)—and not *your*—(without either)—as in the phrase *once in your life*—was the appropriate homonym for the sentence "I hope you're feeling better."

And lest you think the case merely an example of one boy's eccentricity, I assure you that I'm not the only person who suffered this way as a child: Isabelle's sister, Oona, waited impatiently through years of elementary school education for the American history lesson that would at last introduce Richard Stands, whom she knew, though no one ever mentioned him, had to be an essential figure, else why would they have put his name into the Pledge?

(I pledge allegiance to the flag of the United States of America and to the republic for Richard Stands, one nation, under God, with liberty and justice for all.)

"Is that really true?" Gitl Finkelstein says, throwing back her hair and lightly touching my arm. "Oh my God, that's hilarious!"

A vivid sensation, originating in my chest, moves in constricting circles through my solar plexus to my groin, where it coils in upon itself. Leaning towards me, Gitl almost falls and, placing one hand flat against my chest, catches herself, murmuring apologetically in Hebrew, a language I don't understand, but at which I laugh anyway.

"Richard Stands?" she says, and a second jolt courses through me as she rights herself, appraising me while running the zipper of her black leather jacket nervously across the curve of her left breast.

She is exquisitely beautiful, with a strong jawline. Her slightly curving nose holds up a tiny pair of antique eyeglasses and her hair, an explosion of reddish curls, cascades down her shoulders in ringlets, like the spume of a too quickly opened bottle of champagne.

She has come to the department's annual Christmas party, as far as I can tell, without escort or date. Standing with her near the eggnog bowl, I scan the room, but the only person I see watching us is, of course, Isabelle.

Wrapped in an electric-blue shawl, she peers over the shoulder of our department chair, with whom she is ostensibly engaged in rapt conversation.

"WHAT WOMAN?" I say on the drive home. My voice, stilted and artificial, rings hollowly inside the car.

"Near the eggnog bowl. You know: with the hair." Isabelle's voice is equally numb. In fact, we sound like two acting students on the first day of class, our efforts to speak naturally in a scene naturally sabotaging the effect.

"With the hair?" I say, hoping to sound completely befuddled.

"She's attractive, isn't she?" Isabelle asks with a counterfeit nonchalance.

"Gitl, you mean?" I say, as though I could barely place her.

"Is that her name?" Isabelle says, alert to this new datum.

"You find her attractive?" I say, attempting surreptitiously to damage Isabelle's confidence in her own subjectivity, perhaps even causing her to believe that it is she who, in finding Gitl attractive, has displaced her unconscious homoerotic feelings for her onto me.

"Didn't you think so?" Easily she avoids the snare.

"Well, it's very subjective . . ." I allow my voice to trail off as though I had more pressing things to consider.

"All that hair," she sighs, breaking the silence.

"It's a little much." I nod in agreement, as she drives carefully along the icy roads, listening to a tape her sister sent: Elvis Costello and the Chieftans singing about a television set that blows up when the Christmas tree lights are plugged in.

"She's new to your department, isn't she?"

"Gitl, you mean?"

"Or isn't that her name?"

"She played in the Israeli Philharmonic. Trombone, I think. Under Zubin Mehta. At least I think that's what she said."

"That's what you were talking about?"

"Oh, she went on and on. I could hardly get away."

"Hm," Isabelle says, trying to sound, if not bored, then at least uninterested, the gentle interrogation we both know she is conducting inexpertly concealing and revealing itself, and forcing me into this absurd stance of self-parodic befuddlement, my shabby theatricals revealing, as I intend them to conceal, the attraction I'm feeling towards Gitl Finkelstein.

The buildings and the streets are covered in frazzling Christmas lights. Long lines of cars back up along Lamar, waiting to turn onto 38½ Street, where the residents have decked every square inch of their houses and lawns and even the trees that form a canopy over the street with long strings of lights, the wild, lustrous chaos of it all reminding me (quite privately) of Gitl Finkelstein's hair.

I RETURN FROM driving the baby-sitter home to find Isabelle sitting on the sofa, sipping a cup of peppermint tea and staring at the blinking lights of her Christmas tree as they cast their periodic explosions of color against first one wall and then the next.

Before we married and even long afterwards, I refused to allow a tree into the house until one year, near despair, Isabelle cut green and red felt into the shape of a Christmas tree and taped it to the wall of the living room, gathering our presents beneath it. The following year, it was a tiny fir in a planter's pot, no more than a foot high, but tall enough for her to decorate, and by then, of course, the ban was for all practical purposes broken, and in each subsequent year, the tree grew in shape and size, so that every December, I felt further and further oppressed by it.

The pinnacle of this oppression, or rather its nadir — tying a fir to the top of our car as though it were a deer carcass, with Franny, in her excitement, jumping up and down like a caged hyena — was for me a complicated and disturbing act, at once theologically humiliating and socially conformist.

"A Trinitarian godhead is bad enough, but do we really have to rope the trees into it, as well?" I throw my car keys down, too disgusted to even look at the tree, its glittering branches held high like so many arms raised in supplication.

"I was just thinking how beautiful it all is, Charles." Isabelle says this sourly, lifting her teacup to her mouth with both hands in a vain effort to conceal her grimace.

A cache of silver bracelets falls midway to each elbow with a clank.

"A tree has nothing to do with the life of Jesus. You know that, Isabelle, don't you? It's nothing more than pagan, druidical tree worship!"

And this is completely true.

When St. Jerome went out to convert the Druids, he took along an ax. Determined to chop down their holiest tree at the center of their most sacred grove, he wished to demonstrate to the credulous Druids the foolishness of their idolatrous beliefs. The sacred tree was so very large that when it fell, it leveled everything in its path, destroying acres of forest in a crushing avalanche and leaving, as the only survivor of this arboreal holocaust, one small fir.

"And this shall be the Christ tree!" St. Jerome proclaimed to thousands of now confused Druids, no doubt feeling quite pleased with himself. Violence tends to have a salubrious effect on the religious mind, although I must say that now, fifteen hundred years later, as each pious Christian the world over drags a dead fir into his living room and attempts to resurrect it in a pot of water as a dendrological substitution for his slain god, the question remains: who exactly converted whom?

"Because how could a fir tree, Isabelle, have anything to do with a failed messianic coup in the ancient Levant?"

"Well, but if it has nothing to do with either Christianity or Jesus, Charles, then why are you so upset by it?"

(The truth is, St. Jerome ruined practically everything he touched. In his translation of the Book of Isaiah, for instance, his poor Hebrew led him to conflate Nebuchadnezzar, the wicked king of Babylon, with the adversarial angel of the Old Testament, creating the Christian devil Lucifer out of nothing more than the thin air of his deficient vocabulary.)

"I don't care. I don't fucking care about St. Jerome or the Druids or the devil! I don't care about any of it, Charles!" Isabelle says, lowering her voice, remembering that Franny (who, as I say, couldn't be more delighted with the tree) is sleeping in the next room. "It's just a reminder of my childhood, okay? A tree reminds me of not having to go to school, for God's sakes. I mean, why the *fuck* can't you just see it as that and stop attaching all this spurious religious significance to it. I mean, my God, you're worse than the Christians!"

"It's not me, Isabelle. Christmas *is* a religious holiday!"

"Not anymore!" she shouts. "*Now* it's just a secular American holiday celebrating . . . what? . . . I don't know what. Celebrating time off from school. I mean, why can't you just see it as that and just leave me the fuck alone!"

In her fury, she yanks the lights' electrical cord from its socket, plunging our house instantly into darkness.

i can't help thinking of laura mankiewitz

Isabelle brushes her teeth in silence.

She undresses with her back towards me.

She turns off the light on her nightstand without a word before offering me a guttural and disgruntled "Good night" from the other side of the yawning gap that separates her side of the mattress from mine.

I can hardly sleep. Lying awake in bed, I can't help thinking of Laura Mankiewitz. If only she had joined our Sunday school class even a few years earlier, my life might now be entirely different.

Laura, who moved to Karkel with her family in the fourth

grade, transformed the sexual constellation of our little Sunday school class overnight.

Her body was soft with rounding lines, not angular and stick-like like the tomboyish Lizzie Blumgarten's. Her hair, full and frizzy and black, fell in thick hanks over her new breasts, and her face was the face of an angel or at least of a Scandinavian film star.

I was instantly smitten, although, by this time, it was too late.

Three years earlier in public school, on the other side of town, far from our little synagogue with its frosted windows and its rancid old-men smells, I had found my inamorata. Mrs. Appleton had, in fact, assigned her to me as a deskmate. In a naked attempt to divide and conquer the boys, she had split our class on its first day into male-female pairings, seating each couple at a two-person desk, which was then pushed against two other such desks in a sort of T formation, so that three couples now sat and worked at each station.

Below each desktop, between the seats, were two cubbies, one on top of the other. Asking us to behave like the gentlemen she knew we were, Mrs. Appleton instructed the boys to allow the girls to put their Big Chief notepads and their Dutch Masters cigar boxes filled with their fat #7 pencils into the top cubby. Girls were the fairer sex, gentler and more delicate than we, and shouldn't have to bend as low.

I can't speak for the other boys, of course, but I was only too happy to comply with Mrs. Appleton's old-world sense of courtliness, and I graciously deferred the top cubby to my seatmate, Becky Rowan. As she bent down to remove her things from the bottom cubby where she had, on instinct, placed them before I arrived, I was able to gaze for a moment upon her golden brow.

Her hair, the color of lemons, was parted perfectly down the middle, a lily-white seam of scalp running in an unerringly straight line from the top of her forehead to the nape of her neck, pulled out on either side into two shimmering, lutescent ponytails, with little feathery tufts of white hair at the base of her hairline falling like winter grass onto the delicate surface of her bare neck.

She raised her head, the task finished, and smiled at me with a cockle-toothed smile, a large gap where her two front teeth had (perhaps only recently) been.

I couldn't help comparing her to Bridget, Leanne and Lizzie, with disastrous consequences. Too easy assumptions, made that day, imprinted themselves on my green psyche, and Becky Rowan became for me the first in what I can only now describe as a long cavalcade of theologically compromising women, a comely line of beguiling sisters leading ultimately to Isabelle as its climax and summation.

It was thanks to her, I believe, that I became the Jesse Owens of intermarriage in my family, running into the marriage bed of a Gentile woman more quickly than had previously been thought humanly possible.

And just as athletes, in the wake of records once impossible to shatter, were able suddenly to run as swiftly as Owens, so now in my family, I watched with dismay and a growing sense of alarm as uncles and cousins, and even, eventually, my own father in the aftermath of my mother's death, began marrying shiksas left and right, seemingly at every opportunity that presented itself.

It was as though some unwritten quota had been lifted or nullified, and our family, over an inconsiderable number of years, became populated by a growing pocket of Gentile women who lived, as though in a ghetto or township, inside the larger Jewish populace. And through these ghetto walls, each year, they dragged their fragrant Christmas trees. Each year, working without genetic (or apparently even short-term) memory, they purchased boxes of matzah clearly labeled *Not For Passover Use!*

Married now to a Montana mountain woman who towers over his five-foot-four frame, my father dotes on her and her children, giving them gifts of jewelry and stock options, gathering together with them as a family in Kalispell at the end of every year to celebrate a December concoction he charmlessly calls Chanumas.

However, even I have to admit that marrying a Jewess might not have prevented these unfortunate turns. In the December of my fourth-grade year, for instance, I was dismayed to learn that Laura Mankiewitz's father permitted their family a Christmas tree, so that neither Laura nor her sister, he said, would feel in any way culturally deprived.

"It's just a cultural thing," Mr. Mankiewitz said.

However, at the time, it was something no one in my family would have countenanced, and we pitied and despised him for it.

In fact, my sisters and I had subversively constructed for ourselves a counterholiday mythology principally involving a figure we called the Chanukah Man, a sort of anti-Claus who, at least as I imagined him, was clean shaven and thin in a white taffeta yarmulke and a blue taffeta robe. A flowing white tallis shimmering around his neck like a debonair scarf, he trudged on foot from house to house, crossing in eight nights the entire Jewish world, leaving brightly wrapped packages, at least at our house, beneath what we children ironically called our Chanukah Bush, a Star of David constructed out of six yardsticks and covered with crinkled aluminum foil.

Headlights from the street rake across our bedroom wall. I groan and turn over in bed.

Rabbi Kleinblatt once told me that, because matchmaking is so very difficult, God Himself arranges marriages from on high. Trusting neither in His angels nor in mere mortals who would —*as we have done with everything else!*—only make a bedlam of it, God sees to the work Himself, seated atop His throne in the far reaches of a vast Empyrean.

That God, even at this distance, would not arrange marriages contrary to Jewish law is incontrovertible, and if this is true (and why not assume that it is?), it logically follows that somewhere out there, alive in this abject world, is a Jewish woman Heaven has ordained as my wife.

Gitl Finkelstein, perhaps. Or perhaps not.

In either case, I can't help conjuring her face and form again in my mind. I see her standing near the eggnog bowl, but now with her trombone case and a tractate of the Talmud tucked beneath her arm, the sort of woman you might imagine as a pin-up girl on the wall of a yeshiva if the Ashkenazi Jews of the Old World had only had calendars analogous to the ones you sometimes see in Asian grocery stores.

Whoever she is, this figure haunts me.

Staring at the ceiling, I imagine her attending one dreary Jewish singles mixer after another, involving herself in useless, pointless chitchat with pointless, useless men, Zionists and Yiddishists and secularists and dentists, accepting invitation after invitation to weddings and bar mitzvahs, to Shabbos dinners and to brises, to every *simcha,* in fact, on the great revolving wheel of Jewish holidays, hoping to meet me, her intended, her *beshert,* at (at least) one of them, and never finding me there because I am, of course, consorting with a woman forbidden to me by divine law.

Inside the china cabinet she inherited from her bubbe and her zayde, between the Shabbos candlesticks smuggled out of Vilna and the Israeli chanukiah from the time of the '67 war, the delicate figures of a bride and a groom, the ornament from her parents' wedding cake, ages as, un-reused inside the airless case, a webwork of veins advances steadily across it each and every year.

Sitting at a table beneath the cabinet, the Jewess that Heaven has Ordained for Me cries bitterly, throwing herself across the pages of her unfinished dissertation—peering over her shoulder, I glimpse enough of it to see that it concerns Yaakov Emden and his role in the Sabbatean heresy—her reddish curls shaking, her sculpted shoulders sobbing.

And who is to blame for her unhappiness?

Who is to blame?

It would be easy enough to blame Rabbi Kleinblatt and the elders of our community, or even Moses Mendelssohn, whose philosophical heirs they were; easy enough to blame my grandparents, who threw off traditional observance as soon as they stepped off the boat from Europe, as though it were a coat that had somehow caught fire during the crossing.

But this would be unseemly and, in any case, I don't really blame them.

Instead, in the moments of my greatest despondency, though I know it is not just, I blame Mrs. Appleton. Yes! My first-grade teacher. I blame her above all others.

And why? you ask. Why?

Indeed why?

Because: when she sat me next to Becky Rowan and coerced me into gallantly surrendering to her the top cubby, the uses of the word *your* were not the only erroneous thing she unintentionally taught me.

traveling with leibowitz or,
jewish figures in the dreams of richard wagner

Traveling with Leibowitz is like traveling with a child whose
mother has neglected to pack his Ritalin. I've been with him
barely twelve minutes and already I'm exhausted. He has literally not stopped talking since I arrived, encyclopædically re-
hashing every detail of his trip from the minute he left his adoring
wife on their doorstep in Sebastopol to the moment he met me
at the gate, wearing a seersucker suit and a white straw hat identical to mine.

"When I saw you in it earlier this summer at the Shostakovich—and God! what a dreary conference that was, eh?—I had
to have one for myself. You don't mind, of course."

"Of course not," I say, although, of course, I do.

We look ridiculous together, departing customs in our twin suits and matching straw hats, his bottle-green vest, purchased when he was much thinner, straining against his paunch.

(His weight is a legendary subject in our cloistered circle of academic gossip and intrigue. He has been at times Pantagruelian in girth; at other times, merely corpulent; and once, for six months, he was razor thin, even gaunt, thanks to a drastic liquid diet treatment program, at the zenith of which in a moment of unguarded optimism, he gave away his entire wardrobe.)

Now he is as large as I have ever seen him.

And no matter how far I move away from him, he inches near me, standing behind me and pressing his belly into my elbow, purling his honey-toned travelogue into my ear like a cat licking itself with too much affection.

Isabelle and I have often discussed which is the less reprehensible: the overt or the covert narcissist, with Isabelle generally taking the side of the covert narcissist, the narcissist who, because he is at least aware of his own narcissism, is able to compensate for it, if only to a minor degree. Unlike the overt narcissist, the covert narcissist attempts to conceal his narcissism, much in the same way that a person who is missing a tooth will speak with her mouth more tightly drawn than is necessary. Like a merchant luring a customer into his shop with the promise of some free and worthless trinket, the covert narcissist will surrender a small amount of attention to you as a sort of tax he understands he must pay on your larger attentions to him.

Wishing to speak of his own garden, he will ask you, briefly, of yours; on the point of professional promotion, he will inquire into your work, all the while sneaking glances at himself in the mirror or in the darkened window behind you, but only when he is certain you are not watching him, returning his gaze to meet yours a millisecond after your gaze returns to his, so that you can never quite catch him looking away.

At this, the covert narcissist is particularly skilled—although one is always left with the feeling, as he begins to speak at length about his own citronella cuttings or his own new job and its enormous expense account, that his inquiries into yours have been neither genuine nor generous.

And of course, the effect of his eyes ricocheting compulsively between your face and the reflection of his own can be a vertiginous experience, one completely absent from the conversation of the overt narcissist, who, unembarrassed by self-love, has no use for any such masking schemes or stratagems. On the contrary: his narcissism is as raw and unapologetic as an open sewer. Never leaving a verbal gap for anyone else, or no more than is required for an occasional confirming *hunh* or *un-hunh,* the overt narcissist grows listless the moment another person speaks, and the available air in the room diminishes, as even these confirming interjections on the part of his interlocutor grow more perfunctory and strained.

Having thoroughly exhausted his listener's attention, the overt narcissist moves on, without offering conversational compensation of any kind, looking for others before whom he can preen and blather, bragging about one fabled encounter after another with ever greater relish and self-adorning intensity.

I myself become spellbound and mute in the presence of an overt narcissist, listening in vain during his unending recitatif for the momentary cæsura during which, under normal circumstances, I would excuse myself and leave. However, because I am myself (I admit it with some shame) a covert narcissist, there is nothing I can do in the presence of an overt narcissist except, in a kind of simultaneously dizzying and static dance of neurotic compensation, zealously attempt to hide all traces of my own incriminating narcissism, resulting, more often than not, in a virtual paralysis of will.

Because the store of narcissism needed to counter the narcissism of the overt narcissist is so great, the covert narcissist, like a chameleon attempting to hide among chameleons, can only exhaust himself as he seeks to simultaneously affirm and deny the nature of his existence.

And if, in the past, I had been inclined to disagree with Isabelle, to see in the overt narcissist's open acceptance of his own narcissism a gloriously monstrous or heroically Nietzschean assault against the suffocatingly vulgar constraints of a frightened herd mentality (for, after all, is not the covert narcissist doubly—nay, trebly—guilty here, guilty not only of his own narcissism but also of self-hatred *and* of the deviousness required to conceal not only the self-hatred but also the narcissism?), I recant of this opinion now and in the presence of Leibowitz, who, unchastened by either doubt or self-restraint, continues on with his groaning monologue as we enter the airport lobby.

A YOUNG GIRL holding a PROFS. LEIBERT & BELZER sign actually laughs when she sees us approaching her. Greeting us with a graceless shake of her hand, she introduces herself to us as Halina and gestures us through the crowd to the street, where her driver takes our bags, throwing them roughly into the back of a purple Dodge minivan.

I know little Polish, nor the word for *hat* or *buffoon*, but I'm certain they're discussing us, as they maunder away in their native tongue. Seated behind him, I can see the driver looking into his rearview mirror, his pale eyes darting first to an area directly above my head and then to an area directly above Leibowitz's.

The day is hot and the sky cloudless and I have no wish to venture out into it sans chapeau, yet the thought of traveling through dark and gloomy Poland with Leibowitz in these accursed straw hats, like two Jewish vaudevillians on a summer tour, is, frankly, more than I can bear. We resemble a kitschy pair of salt and pepper shakers. And if I remove my hat, placing it as nonchalantly as I can upon my left knee, Leibowitz also removes his, placing it on his right knee; if I casually return mine to my head, Leibowitz also quite casually throws his back on.

Defeated, I simply stare out the window, as Leibowitz continues holding court, leaning back in his seat, like a pasha, against the soft pillows of his own plump back, angling his body towards me, rolling his eyes and his *R*s.

And if I allow my eye to wander, even for a moment, from his face, to the window to take in the city, his voice changes, growing insistent, more pointed and completely impossible to either ignore or avoid.

"Hunh," is all I can say.

"Un-hunh."

"En, em-hmn."

"Yes," I say, raging inside the prison of my own silence, until even these meaningless promptings become difficult to articulate.

"And these others?" I manage to finally preempt him. "The ones you mentioned in your letter. Will they be joining us at the train station? Or at the hotel in Kraków, I suppose?"

"Oh, no. No, no, Belski. We'll be seeing them only at the conference, I'm afraid."

"Only at the conference?"

"Yes, apparently none of them had the heart for it," he says, and my own heart, entering the conversation if only by inference, sinks.

• • •

A BILIOUS CLOT OF panic rises to the back of my throat.

Although Leibowitz is one of the most brilliant of my colleagues, I've tended to avoid him in the past. His intellect is daunting, prodigious, and this, combined with an infantile need for attention, makes him, at best, an exhausting companion.

When he wrote to me, as he did to others, that in order to fully comprehend the Wagner conference, we should first come to Auschwitz, I never for a moment considered going. In a later note, however, when he mentioned that several of the conference participants, many quite prominent in our field, had agreed to join him on "this dour pilgrimage," I reconsidered, thinking perhaps their company might make the journey worthwhile, after all.

And how difficult could it be to avoid Leibowitz, I reasoned, even in a smallish crowd?

Purring unctuously, he looks at me with an exaggerated affection, as a benevolent monarch might his wayward liege. He strokes the little grey beard hanging like a trowel from the plinth of his chin.

"We don't need those others, do we, Belski? Emm? We'll be fine without them, hey?"

THE RADIO PLAYS an uninflected stream of Euro-pop. On a billboard outside, a man and a woman make love on top of an office copy machine. As we near the city center, the facades of buildings grow bright with colorful ads and signs in a post-Glasnost Esperanto: COCA-COLA . . . PANASONIC . . . SONY . . . SEXSHOP . . . MASAZ. It's as though the Invisible Hand of Market Capitalism has doodled all over the city in English.

The main thing, I tell myself, is *not* to get off the van.

Instead, I will calmly ask the driver to return me to the airport, where I will trade in my ticket for an earlier flight to Germany, heedless of the cost. If he can't take me or if, for some reason, he won't—perhaps his schedule is too tight or he has another fare, although where would he be going now other than to the airport?—it's simple enough to catch a cab from the train station.

I suppose I should offer an at-least plausible excuse to Leibowitz. However, at the moment, I can think of none. Which is entirely his fault. Had he informed me earlier about the others, I could have bowed out gracefully, sparing us both, because the truth is, the tedium of his company aside, there is something terrifying about simply *being in Poland.* I feel as though I were being dragged back to the scene of my own murder. And as embarrassing as it is to admit, I'm aware that on some irrational level I'm literally afraid that at the sight of us standing before them on their land, some atavistic mechanism in the basal brain of the Poles we encounter on the street will fire, transforming them instantly into a murderous mob, compelled (perhaps even against their own sweet reason and will) into performing one final pogrom on Leibowitz and myself, as though fifty years of history and the Communist debacle had not passed and it were still 1945.

So pervasive is this antique view that I actually imagined all Polish women, even the younger ones, would be lumpish, sexless columns in babushkas and black widow's smocks, indistinguishable from one another except by the number of wens on their faces. (Instead, many of them, as I see clearly outside our van windows, are stunningly attractive, slender in light summer dresses, stylish in an almost Parisian way.)

Not more than an hour ago, as my plane descended over vibrant green farmland and I peered through its little window, breathing in and out of my airsickness bag in the hope of staving off the worst of my anxieties, I was taken aback to see that Poland is actually *in color* and not locked eternally somehow in the black-and-white duotones of all those grainy photographs of massacres and atrocities Rabbi Kleinblatt and my religious teachers so conscientiously supplied to us, the children in their charge, as though our feeling sick to our stomachs was the best way to impress upon us the uniqueness of the Jewish people and the power of the God who had chosen us as His own.

"Daddy, hey, Daddy!" Franny whispered to me last Christmas morning, sitting on her knees so she could see the screen when, in a preemptive move against the rising yuletide, I took her to a double-feature of Yiddish movies at the local art house. "Is it just the film they used," she wanted to know, "or did the whole world used to be in black and white?"

"Both, Franny," I lied, although the irony was lost on her, of course.

I'd purchased two subscriptions to the week-long series, in the hope of persuading Gitl Finkelstein to accompany me. However, she was spending the holiday in silent retreat at a zendo in Western Massachusetts with her fiancé, Albedrío Montez, a radical Episcopal theologian, and so I took Franny and sometimes even Isabelle with me instead. Except for a passel of querulous old men in caps and a few fanatic cinéastes, we were often the only ones there.

Franny had trouble with the subtitles, of course. And in retrospect, why I imagined a handful of obscure films acted in a dead language by forgotten stars for a public whose culture no longer exists could entice her into identifying with her heritage is beyond even me. Isabelle, however, seemed to enjoy herself and was even moved to tears.

With her cowboy boots on the chair in front of her and a cappuccino in a paper cup warming her hands, she dug into her coat pocket for a crumpled tissue and loudly blew her nose during the antic climax of *Yidl mitn Fidl,* when Yidl (played by the incomparable Molly Picon) reveals to the handsome Froim (Leon Liebgold) that she is not the lad he thought.

"Sha! Kvyet!" The old men behind us raised their angry canes, as the half-light cast by the vintage neon clock, with the words COOL REFRESHING AIR CONDITIONING spelled out in a blue ring around it, was caught, sparklike, in Isabelle's tears.

"It's just so sad," she whispered, clutching at my arm. "A whole world was lost, Belski, or don't you feel that?"

"BELSKI, ARE YOU COMING?" Leibowitz roars, standing on the sidewalk outside the train station, two dark half-moons of perspiration staining the underarms of his jacket. He lifts his straw hat and daubs at his bald pate with a handkerchief, the morning light glinting off his forehead in two solar coins. His face is ashen and strained by petulance, his cheeks are stubbled blue-grey around the edged rim of his goatee.

Clinging to the sliding door of the van, I gaze down at him and, in that moment, I realize with a sudden and certain fury that he has lied to me. Our colleagues hadn't changed their minds. They never agreed to come here with him in the first place. Like myself, none of them would have dreamed of traveling with Leibowitz; unlike myself, however, they were not sufficiently naïve to assume that any of us would have felt otherwise.

"Are you stepping down, Professor Belzer?"

The driver has handed Leibowitz his bag and now holds mine expectantly; Halina stands nearby, paying no attention to my hesitations, nosing through our itinerary; Leibowitz impatiently taps his cane; and I want to thunder down at them all, hurling accusations and insisting upon my right to return to the airport immediately, immediately!

But I don't, of course.

I can't.

It's difficult to explain, but as I look down at him, at Leibowitz, at this poor fellow, a victim of his own unfortunate personality, and think of him actually having to lie in order to procure a companion for this trip, I'm involuntarily flooded with a sympathy and a pity for him against which I'm helpless to defend myself. Even if I could defend myself against it, I doubt I possess sufficient social courage to back out now. Instead, I climb from the van and take my bag, lifting its pull bar and rolling it along behind me, following Halina's bouncing ponytail into the dark corridors of the Warsaw train station.

we return to marszałkowska street

Having stowed our bags, we return to Marszałkowska Street, where the inexplicable empathy I felt for Leibowitz moments before evaporates. Every second now is exquisitely painful. In a private agony, my hands balled into tight fists, my sphincter constricting, I troop along behind them in a state of anæsthetized dreaming, like an Australian bushman forced onto someone else's walkabout.

There is no airport in Kraków, and so we have flown into Warsaw and will take a train there, and now, with more than two hours to kill, Leibowitz suggests a visit to the Museum of Caricatures ("The satirical portraits by Lipinski," he insists, "are not to be missed!") or to the Jewish Cemetery ("Where I will show you Zamenhof's tomb, Belski, the great L. L. Zamenhof, the inventor of Esperanto, a typical Polish Jew, dreaming of a typically Jewish utopia, its one requirement being that every man speak a language foreign to himself— *Ha!*").

But, thankfully, Halina demurs. "It's a bit of a walk," she says, eying Leibowitz, who, in truth, looks in no shape for an extended urban hike. His hair, matted with perspiration, is curling into tiny rings, its dye seemingly dripping down his neck. Besides, she says, she's uncertain if the museum or the cemetery are open today or at this hour, and instead suggests a simple tour of the Palace of Culture.

A gift from Stalin to the Polish people, the Palace rises ponderously above us, directly across the street, dominating the skyline, each of its four heavy turrets, at the base of its huge central column, lined by a rim of jagged spires.

After the collapse of the Soviet Union, Halina says, the Polish people didn't quite know what to do with this oppressive gift and considered tearing it down. They didn't, she says, but only because the best views of the city are from its top floors.

"The best views—emm?—are from its top floors, yes?" Leibowitz coos, trying to keep up with her as she marshals us across the street.

"*Tak, tak,* because from there, you see, you cannot see Palace of Culture!"

"Ah! Aha!" Leibowitz rubs his plump hands together in a

display of feigned delight. "The ironies, the ironies!" he roars, and Halina blushes, pleased at the boldness of her little joke and its success.

The main thing, I tell myself, is *not* to get on the train.

As soon as I have reclaimed my bag, I will make whatever excuses I must in order to hail a cab and disappear into the thick traffic on Marszałkowska Street, returning to the airport and escaping to Germany, before either Halina or Leibowitz can raise a hand to stop me.

in the lobby of the palace of culture

In the lobby of the Palace of Culture, there is no attendant inside the glass ticket booth and, after twenty minutes or so of tedious waiting, we decide to walk the grounds, looking for a place to have a drink.

A dingy smog hangs above the marketplace. Large black and white banners announcing a *Godo* by Beckett and a play by *Shikspir* hang limply above our heads. On the front decks of a bar nearby, a wiry man, his biceps bulging, sweeps last night's debris into discrete piles. He looks us over, staring at our hats, and without demonstrable regret, informs Halina that he is not yet open for the day.

We sit on a low wall and consider our choices.

"It doesn't have to be a bar," Leibowitz says, raising his eyebrows flirtatiously. "A *napój bezalkoholowy* would do."

Smarmily, he's attempted to draw her out, I've noticed, smiling at her patiently translated answers to his haltingly translated questions. Practicing Polish phrases from a little phrase book he keeps in his breast pocket, he has quizzed her on usage and meaning, rehearsing pronunciations and giggling at her schoolmarmish corrections.

Now, he searches its tiny pages for the words *przekąska* and *napój,* repeating each several times, while Halina giggles, pronouncing the syllables to herself, with Leibowitz egging her on until, finally admitting defeat, he simply shows her the book, pointing at the words, his long thumbnail creasing its page.

"Ah! *Przekąska i napój!*"

"Yes!" he halloos.

"But why didn't you say so?"

Rising happily, she leads us to an outdoor café on a concrete island near one of the Palace's many parking lots, where the unpleasant smells of diesel fumes mingle with Leibowitz's florid cologne.

I excuse myself from the table, offering to buy the drinks, and when I return a moment later, the glasses riding on the necks of their bottles, Leibowitz and Halina are deep in conversation.

"Oh, but of course, of course!" She is almost singing to him.

"Ah, my dear Halina."

"Yes, my dear Professor?"

"One more question, if I may?" He strokes his little beard before launching into his next question. After only two sips of soda, his vest, I notice, is already dotted with a light sprinkling of Diet Pepsi. He leans in towards her.

"What . . . emmm," he says in a presumptuously intimate tone, "what, I'm wondering, do Poles . . . ehhh . . . generally think of . . . Jews today?"

"Of . . . Jews?" she says.

"Leibowitz," I caution him.

"Yes, you see, Professor Belzer and I are . . . um, um, um . . . Jews." His soft fist curls first towards his own chest, then, falling backwards and opening into a finger, points at mine.

Halina follows his hand, frowning, as though it weren't entirely polite for her to believe what he has just told her. She looks at the two of us and then at our hats, as though finally understanding a riddle she could not previously solve. She shrugs.

"Most like them, I think, but some don't, but these—they don't like Chinese or niggers, either."

"Niggers?" Leibowitz says.

"Em, *tak*," Halina nods, sipping at her lemon tonic through a straw.

"Well," I say, on the point of standing, when, as though summoned by Leibowitz's confession (which he might as well have shouted from the church tops!) a dirty man in a filthy checkered shirt and checkered pants is suddenly at our table.

I'd noticed him earlier, sitting on a concrete ledge nearby, watching us, his face a reddened drunkard's face, his silver hair, cut convict-short, bristling like a hedgehog's quills. Leaning his hands on our table, he looms over us, pressing the weight of his upper body onto his gnarled fingers, his shirt partially open and misbuttoned, so that I can see the sweating humps of his sagging chest inside it.

Here at last, I think, is the Poland I'd expected, and I brace myself for the worst; but before he can even finish a sentence, Halina is standing also, bristling as well, shooing him away and hurling a torrent of Polish invective onto his head. He sneers, attempting to argue with her, but at the same time, I notice, he flinches and has already begun to skulk away.

"He'll only use it for vodka for sure," Halina says, as the man returns to his ledge, where, sitting exactly as he had before, he appraises our table, as though he has already forgotten the encounter and is considering approaching us (again) for the first time, trying to determine whether he will be rebuked or chased away.

And then, it's as though an invisible path had been cleared to our table, and a gypsy woman is, as suddenly, standing on its other side. Clinging to two filthy children, one an infant in her arms, she holds a dried-out baby bottle in the same hand as her begging cup, thrusting both beneath my nose.

The stench of rancid formula is overwhelming and my head swims inside its sweetly wretched reek.

"Don't!" Halina shrieks as I reach for my wallet, and the gypsy woman shrieks back, and Halina shrieks at the gypsy woman and not hysterically, either, as the woman has, but brusquely in a businesslike manner, as though she were a receptionist ordering a vagrant from an office lobby.

Withdrawing my hand, I stare at my drink on the concrete table, but the woman refuses to leave, hovering above us like an avenging angel, scorning Halina with her every gesture, twisting the baby's head this way and that, her hand a horseshoe gripping its chin, exhibiting the scars and scabs that decorate its tiny face.

By the time we retrieve our bags from the dingy cloakroom where we left them, I'm exhausted. We tip the little crumpled man who works there the smallest amount, on Halina's recommendation. Like a deep-sea crustacean scuttling across the ocean floor, he moves between the high stacks of bags in the back room and his grimy desk in front without either raising his shoulders or removing his cigarette. Squinting through the smoke that rises from his mouth like a series of veils, he waves after us with a fragile, papery hand, calling: *"Dziękuję, dziękuję bardzo!"*

Descending more deeply into the labyrinth of concrete hallways, we trudge past travelers hauling their cases, their faces sickly green beneath the poor fluorescent lighting. Black-and-white signs above escalators flash place names that seem fantastical to me: Lublin, Białystok, Katowice.

By the time Halina brings us to Platform 4, Leibowitz is sweating uncontrollably. His small head is red and flushed. Huffing, he places his heavy bag onto the ground, removing his hat and wiping his forehead with a blue silk kerchief.

The place is a whirl of energy. Slavic-faced boys in red, white and blue rapster threads run freewheeling figure-eights in and out of the crowds gathering here. The gypsy woman returns with another gypsy woman, each surrounded at the knee by a vibrant skirt of clinging children who, breaking off from their mothers, run through the crowd, skipping and playing and begging for cash.

At the sight of them, one man picks up his valise and moves off. Another looks down in disgust, and a third approaches me, dressed in khaki shorts and a striped knit shirt with little golden Camel cigarette insignias sewn into it: an American, I presume. Stocky, in a ball cap, with a grizzled blond-grey beard lying like a blanket across his flabby chin, he addresses me in Polish, pointing curiously at my hat and at Leibowitz's, and although Halina is the only one of us to respond to him, he ignores her, directing his words exclusively at me, as though I were an actor in a film she's dubbing.

His intrusion into our circle has thrown my timing off completely. I had been looking for the precise moment during which I could beg off from the trip, and now, before I can even clear my throat or find the words to extricate myself, a train has roared in, its presence galvanizing the crowd, who pick up their cases and shuffle them to no discernible advantage.

"No, here, look, Professor Belski, here is your train," Halina cries, as another rumble approaches and another train roars in and another electric current courses through the crowd, occasioning the same pointless shifting of baggage, the same preparatory adjustment of clothing. As sweaters are buttoned and unbuttoned, ties loosened and unloosened, hats adjusted or removed, I think to myself: Who am I kidding? I can't even chase a beggar from a table. What possible hope do I stand against as formidable an opponent as a Leibowitz?

There is no way out or back. The moment, if ever there was a moment, for liberating myself has passed and I know it. As though in a dream, I heft my bag and move behind Leibowitz through the moving crowd towards the train, until we are inside it, with Halina following along outside. I watch her disappearing and appearing in each of the train's windows as we move down its corridor. Finally, she stops outside a compartment and, gesturing energetically, indicates that these are our seats, her muffled voice sounding through the glass as though she were trapped inside a well.

She will wait here with us, she shouts, until the train departs.

"It's! not! necessary!" Leibowitz shouts back at her.

"Thank! you! thank! you! anyway!" I shout at her, as well.

Although, in fact, neither of us is actually shouting. From the other side of the glass, it might appear that we are shouting, but actually, we are simply hurling frantically whispered phrases towards her, exaggerating our expressions and opening our mouths as wide as possible.

She pantomimes to us that we should sit and I realize we have been standing, like gentlemen, waiting for her to sit first. We obey her, removing our jackets and loosening our ties and placing our suitcases on flat metal shelves above each other's heads.

Leibowitz removes his hat and, standing again, places it upside down on top of his suitcase, his girth filling the small space between us, so that I have to turn my head not to find my nose buried in his crotch. Then I stand and, removing my own hat, place it on top of my suitcase on the shelf above his head. He mops his brow with his silk kerchief. Enfolding his beard inside the cloth and, squeezing it, he wrings out the moisture.

Halina hovers outside the window, not more than a foot from us but sealed off completely by its green-tinted glass. I worry that she may stand there, if not forever, then at least until our train pulls out, a blur in my peripheral vision, an eternal witness to my utter abjection; but satisfied her duty has been performed, she finally points to the bank of escalators behind her, indicating that she will now leave.

But before she can go, Leibowitz slips a small camera out of his jacket and, holding it near his chin, as though it were a prize on a game show, he gestures dramatically towards it, requesting a souvenir photo.

Halina blushes, posing insecurely, bashfully, though flattered nonetheless, as the flash fills our compartment with its nervous scatterings of light.

We bow again and nod, pantomiming our gratitude to her, whispering "Thank! you! thank! you!" through the glass, our expressions exaggerated, like two mimes at the end of a dreary performance.

ineluctably metaphorical

There is something ineluctably metaphorical about riding a train in Poland, although perhaps only for a Jew.

Outside our window, the day is calm and serene. Bluebonnets line the track; women with hoes work the fields; a boy dashes along beside us, racing the engine. In the distance, an old woman ambles up a path; two elderly men stroll arm in arm in the opposite direction; while Leibowitz and I trundle over the same tracks that ferried our grandparents and our great-grandparents and our aunts and our uncles and our cousins and their friends and their neighbors and even the strangers they lived among to their deaths in Auschwitz 300 kilometers away.

It's impossible to even *see* this country, the actual Poland. Its metaphorical twin, I realize, possesses too strong a grip upon my mind. I consider pretending to be asleep in order to avoid discussing this or any other phenomenon with Leibowitz, but no sooner have I closed my eyes than he thunders out: "My God, what a bitch! Or I suppose you didn't think so, Belski?"

I open my eyes and find his little bald head staring at me, its goatee thrust martially forward.

"Is it not enough they took our houses, our businesses and our lives? Must they have our tourist dollars as well!"

"Emm, emm, emm?" he says, tweaking his little mustache, so pleased is he to have regained my attention. "I mean, who does she think she is, denying us this rare visit to the Museum of Caricatures or to Zamenhof's tomb so that we could—what?—sit in that horrid little café of hers, listening to her rehearse her racist theories, pestered by vagrants, to whom she refused even the slightest help, while insisting at the same time that *you* treat *her* for the drinks *she* forced upon *us*."

Swelling in a theatrical rage, he threatens to inform Halina's superiors. "Not that they'll care. Of course, they won't. They despise us and have for a thousand years!" The Church is implicated. "Because it was the Church that stirred up their peasants' minds against us—didn't it?—with this trumped-up charge of deicide when it was *they* who killed God, Belski—yes, the *Christians* killed God!—God the Father, rendering him obsolete and replacing him with this new and improved god, this newfangled *human* god. And what could they do with their guilt over *that* except project it onto us Jews for a thousand years of *goyim nakhes,* a thousand years of fun and sport!"

Even here, beneath the dull electric bulbs, the two coins of reflected light radiate off his skull.

"I'll tell you one thing," he roars, his heels raised and his thighs jerking up and down like pistons. "This is the absolute last time I allow Mrs. Leibowitz to make my travel arrangements for me!"

"No, not my wife, Belski!" His squalling face crumples up like a discarded sheet of paper. "Do you actually think I call my wife 'Mrs. Leibowitz'? Of course not. I'm referring to my mother." He presses his kerchief against his wrinkled brow. "*Mon Dieu!* There must be at least three levels of middlemen involved in our every move: there's Mrs. Leibowitz, there's her friend the travel agent, the Polish agents, the car dispatchers. Even the hotel, I'm certain, receives a kickback. I mean, what are we—*what are we, Belski?*—but small, necessary cogs in a great machine designed only for the purpose of extracting money from us?"

Here, I take a moment to offer the Polish woman who had earlier entered our compartment another in a series of hurried and apologetic glances. She merely scowls into her book, her hair cascading down her shoulders in blonde swaths.

"You do that a lot, don't you?" Leibowitz's eyes narrow accusingly. "This ogling of attractive women. Yes, *alles meydlekh zaynen sheyn* for you, I couldn't help noting, even in our small time together. Out the van window! In the train station! In the street! At the café! It's a regular vaudeville with you, isn't it, performed everywhere as though you were—what?—a judge in an international beauty pageant of some kind. *Ha!*"

"*Przepraszam, Pani!*" he shouts at the woman, one clawed hand clutching his little phrase book, the other awkwardly forcing his reading glasses onto his nose. "*Czy mówi po angielsku?*"

"*Nie, nie.*" She shakes her head with a pleasant petulance before returning to the enviable solitude of her book.

"Ah. There. You see, Belski. She doesn't even speak English. *Votre petit secret, votre peu de fétiche* is safe with me. I'm not criticizing you, of course. I merely asked clinically, wondering what effect all this casual voyeurism has on your wife."

PERHAPS BECAUSE OF THIS time spent with Leibowitz, I've begun to dread the conference in Bayreuth, the endless hours of academic pontification over the old Wagnerian conundrum of art and its maker: can a rascal and a mountebank create a noble work?

Wagner, of course, was an overt narcissist, a veritable encyclopædia of calamitous personality traits. Vain, pretentious, hypocritical, hypersensitive, he was a dandy and a fop. A debtor who seduced the wives of his friends and the daughters of his benefactors, he impregnated the future Frau Wagner while she was still married to the conductor Von Bülow, all the while importuning the poor man to stage his *Gesamtkunstwerke,* those ponderously (and, unfortunately for us, heartbreakingly) beautiful musical dramas.

In conversation, he was obsessive and monological. A typical Wagner harangue could last from six to eight hours, and if he caught his friends or guests in conversations of which he was neither the topic nor the center, he would open his mouth and, full-lunged, call forth an inarticulate scream.

Without irony, he considered the world premiere of his *Ring of the Nibelung* "the most important event in the history of human civilization." And yet, he was sensitive to slight and even published a long work entitled *A Dictionary of Insults Containing Terms of Abuse, Derision, Hostility and Slander which have been used against the Master Richard Wagner, his Works and his Supporters by his Enemies and Detractors.*

In addition to the seven operas and their libretti for which he is justifiably famous, he was, in his spare time, a racial theorist and a shrill social critic who cranked out tracts against vivisection and cockfighting. An early proponent of animal rights, he was, not unlike his latter-day acolyte Adolf Hitler, a politicized vegetarian who believed that eating meat poisoned the blood.

Perhaps the vilest of his pamphlets is the essay *Judaism in Music.* Published anonymously originally and only later under his own name, the essay bemoans, in Wagner's phrase, the "be-Jewing of modern art": "Innately incapable of announcing himself to us artistically through either his outward appearance or his speech and least of all through his singing"—which, elsewhere, he describes as "incoherent synagogue gurgling"—"the Jew," according to Wagner, cannot make art, but only glue together, as "a mannered bric-a-brac," fragmented pieces of two thousand years of European art and culture, never mind Heine, Meyerbeer or Offenbach.

Simultaneously a physically repulsive former cannibal *and* the bad conscience of modern civilization (having forced his crippling sense of ethics down the throat of Europe's once happy pagans in the form of a repressive Christianity), the Jew, for Wagner, is redeemable only through "total destruction."

"All Jews should be burned at a performance of *Nathan the Wise*," the composer suggests over coffee one morning to his wife, Cosima, who, as an act of spousal piety, records the injunction in her diary.

And while it may be overstating the case to blame the destruction of European Jewry on one egomaniacal tunesmith—still, one would have to divorce art and culture from the political life of nations, as Wagner's tin-eared apologists do, to deny the effect of his theorizing upon the popular imagination, buoyed, as it was, by the authority of his universally acclaimed art—what *can* be stated without contradiction is that if it weren't for Wagner, *I* certainly wouldn't be stuck on this train heading for Auschwitz with Leibowitz. Intrigued by the paradoxical complexities of Wagner's mind, I published a small article not long ago entitled "Jewish Figures in the Dreams of Richard Wagner," an expanded version of which I've been invited to deliver at this year's Bayreuth conference (its theme: "Wagner and the Jews") and the sole copy of which Leibowitz appears to be holding in his hands when I return to our compartment after a long stay in the club car.

"It was in your briefcase," he explains, "which I discovered was not properly latched."

"Locked," he corrects himself. "Did I say *latched*? I meant *locked*."

"No need to thank me, dear boy. I had nothing to do while you were away, after all, and so I said to myself, 'Belzer, Belzer, *lama sabachthani?*' Just kidding. I said to myself, 'Leibert, Leibert, why not review Belzer Belzer's work, as a sort of favor to him,' you know, a senior colleague showing an avuncular interest in the work of a younger man, because as it's said, as you know, '*Emes iz nor bay Gott, un bay mir, a bissel.*'"

He opens its pages, which he has creased down the middle, and I see that he has marked his comments all over them in a squat red pen. Paragraphs are circled and hatched, sentences crossed out and written over. Asterisks and arrows litter the margins as though they had been jotted upon by a daydreaming football coach.

"*L'essai est très bon, très bon, oui, oui, vraiment.*" He flips through its pages, his pen behind his ear. "This recapitulation of Wagner's dreams is very good, very clear, yes . . ."

As one might expect, the dreamscape of Wagner's mind was no less bedeviled by Jews than was his waking consciousness. In one dream, for instance, recorded by Cosima in the diaries,

Wagner attends a meeting at a synagogue, where he is ceremonially greeted by "two powerfully muscular Jews." In another, he's molested by "two importunate Jewesses," and in a third, dreamed by Cosima herself, he's murdered—"by a Jew," it goes without saying.

"Hmn, yes, you employ Jung's compensatory theory of dream images to fine effect here, Belski: the muscular Jews compensating for Wagner's waking conception of Jews as weak and physically reprehensible; the seductive Jewesses for Wagner's inability to eroticize a dark other. And yet, it's nothing we've not seen before, perhaps not in the case of Wagner, but in general; it's a pretty tired move, don't you think?"

Grinning, Leibowitz bares his teeth. He sucks on the bow of his glasses, as though searching for the correct phrase.

"The thing is, my dear boy, the thing you neglect to mention . . . and . . . and which I think is certainly *at least* as interesting as, if not *more interesting,* than your thesis is that Jung himself had experiences of this kind, dream experiences—yes—not unlike Wagner's, in fact, stemming in part, I think it's fair to say, from his Oedipal resentments towards his mentor Freud, which allowed him to take the wrong side on many an issue of the day."

Here, Leibowitz brings up Jung's disastrous essay "The State of Psychotherapy Today," in which the Swiss psychoanalyst attempts to delineate the differences between an "Aryan psychology" and its "Jewish counterpart."

"*This* in 1934, Belski."

But even as early as 1918, in an essay entitled "The Role of the Unconscious," Jung had already tarred the so-called Jewish psyche with the shabbiest code words of his day, characterizing it as "nomadic," "rootless," "parodic" and "incapable of creating a cultural form of its own."

"And I quote!" Leibowitz bellows, apparently reciting from memory. " 'Jews are physically weaker, like women, and so must aim at the chinks in their opponents' armor,' Jung writes — conveniently forgetting that it is Freud the Jew and not Jung the good Swiss burgher who has created psychoanalysis and, in creating psychoanalysis, has created the modern world. And that now, in 1934"—he jabs his finger at my chest—"with the Nazi *hunde* purging German society of its undesirable Jewish elements, it is Jung himself, specifically in the opportunistic timing of his attack, who is aiming at the chinks in *his* opponent's armor, in Freud's armor!"

Rolling up his sleeves, Leibowitz places my paper between his teeth. "Mnrjfkmnrdmdrrlfmghjnrwhfmdnf . . ." he says, before removing the manuscript from his mouth and leaving an impression of his dentures along its top margin. ". . . but these are only a few of several public instances of what might be called Jung's famous antisemitic pique, and it interests us, Belski, as scholars—not as Jews, mind you, but as scholars—only in so far as it throws light on his subsequent dream life."

He caresses the bottoms of his mustaches with a manicured nail.

"Late in the 1950s, as you surely know, Jung suffered a nearly fatal heart attack, and as he hovered between life and death in his hospital room, he experienced a series of dreams or, more properly speaking, visions: hypnagogic or hypnopompic, I can't remember which is which. Which is which, Belski? Hynopompic or hypnagogic? Ehh? No matter. In either case, these visions, these imaginings of a phrensied delirium had a peculiarly Jewish cast to them. Not only did the feverish Jung envision himself being cared for by an ancient Jewish nurse who fed him ritually kosher foods, but he imagined himself, as well, later at a wedding in the fabled Garden of Pomegranates, where, in utter bliss, he was, at times, the groom himself, Shimon bar Yochai, the Talmudic adept thought by the credulous of our people to be the author of the mystical *Zohar*— can you imagine?—and at other times merely as a privileged guest, a witness to what the Christians call the *coniunctio spirituum* and what our Jewish mystics, in their earthier Hebrew, describe as the marriage of *Tiferet* and *Malchut,* the masculine and feminine aspects of God."

Leibowitz grows even more animated, if that's possible. "Consider it, Belski. Here's Jung, originally as antisemitic as Wagner and yet, exactly like Wagner, entering a highly Judaicized world in his dreams! Surpassing Wagner as a mystic, however, Jung experiences the highest revelation that Jewish mystical thought can provide. For what is the marriage of *Tiferet* and *Malchut* but the joining of all apparent opposites—light and darkness, male and female, Heaven and Earth, God and Israel, either and or—in an eternal embrace, making one indistinguishable from the other!

"It's too delicious, no? It is, it is! It's delicious and it *must* be incorporated into your treatise! A more thorough examination is called for! Take some notes, for God's sakes!" Raising his index finger, Leibowitz points to the heavens. "Or am I simply blathering to the ethers?"

Merely to placate him, I remove a pen and a small notebook from my pocket and pretend to take notes.

"*Sie dürfen Eckermann zu meinem Goethe spielen,*" he says, his hands pressed flat together beneath his chin, his eyes scanning the ceiling of our compartment, as though in search of inspiration. "Now I'm thinking here specifically of Freud and his well-known fascination with Michelangelo's *Moses.* You see, Belski, interestingly enough, it's here that Freud's own latent antisemitic self-loathing comes to the fore. Freud, who was not named Sigmund originally—Did you not know this?—but rather Siegmund, by a mother who, like many a cultured Jewess in German-speaking countries during the 1850s, named her son after a character in"— here, he trumpets out a brief phrase from *Die Walküre* —"Wagner, Belski, Wagner!"

According to Leibowitz, it's Michelangelo's phantasmagorically brawny *Moses* with its (in Freud's words) "giant frame and tremendous physical power" that becomes, for Freud, an emblematic idealization of "the Jew."

"Or perhaps only of the German Jew, the Jew of Western Europe, for, like Wagner, Freud abhorred what he perceived as the delicate and effeminate Eastern European Jew, the unassimilated yid. As with Wagner, so with Freud: the physically weak and therefore repulsive Jew is transformed by the unconscious mind into a colossus, in Freud's case the *Moses* with its Nordic brow and its forearms as large as fucking footballs! Talk about your Freudian wish fulfillment, Belski! I mean, you certainly don't grow forearms like that hauling around tractates of the Gemara, do you? No, you most certainly do not! HA! And yet, *mein Gott.* Even Herzl —even Theodor Herzl, the father of Zionism, negotiating at the end of the nineteenth century with the Sultan of Turkey and the Kaiser of Germany for the restoration of Palestine as a Jewish state—was guilty of this 'family prejudice,' let's call it, Belski, this Jewish antisemitism, this Yiddish self-loathing.

"They were neighbors, did you realize that? Herzl and Freud: neighbors, yes, living at 19 and 6 Berggasse in Vienna, respectively. Strange, isn't it?" he murmurs. . . . "Isn't it strange? Two of the century's most controversial social movements hatched on the same narrow street!"

He takes a deep breath.

"And did you know that before he conceived of the idea of a Jewish state as the cure for the incurable disease of European antisemitism, Herzl's original plan involved the collective conversion of all of Europe's Jews in a mass ceremony at Vienna's St. Stephen's Cathedral, a plan he gave up on, in part, only because the Pope refused to meet with him about it.

"I mean, my God, Belski, here is Herzl—Herzl, the fucking father of Zionism—as reprehensible an antisemite as Wagner, having clearly written in his diaries that the embarrassing and unassimilated Eastern European Jew was of an entirely different race from the enlightened and evolved German Jew. *Race,* Belski! *Race!* That *is* the word he used! And is it really such a coincidence then that both Hitler and Herzl, as though they were somehow complementary dream figures in a slumbering Europe's vast unconscious mind, conceived of their life's work while listening to"—this time, he announces a phrase from *Die Götterdämmerung*—"Wagner's operas!

"Ah-Aha!" he screams. "Isn't that remarkable?"

And closing his eyes, he appears to quote from memory: "'It was only on those evenings when there was no Wagner performed at the Opera that I was assailed by doubts as to the validity of my own ideas,' Herzl recounts in his diaries at the time he was writing his pamphlet 'The Jewish State.'

"The teenaged Hitler, Belski, young Schickelgruber, according to his trusted friend Kubizek, was so transformed by a performance of Wagner's *Rienzi* that he was unable to speak for hours, his eyes feverish with excitement, and when he finally found his voice, he spoke in a state of complete ecstasy of a special mission that would one day be entrusted to him to lead his people out of servitude and to the heights of freedom.

"And isn't it remarkable, Belski, that in both cases, Hitler's *and* Herzl's, each man's life's work specifically involved the utter and ineradicable removal of Jews from the European continent!"

He slams his hand down repeatedly upon the seat's plastic arm rest.

"Now *that! that! that! that!,* my friend, *that* is the real theme of your discourse, one which no one has yet explored! Think of it: the Jew, the nightmare terror of all of dreaming Europe. I mean, what was so frightening about this little Eastern European yid, this *Ostjude,* with his soft hands and his ringling earlocks, with his caftan and his skullcap, that these great men—and they were great men: scientists, artists, statesmen, mass murderers— were afraid to look in the mirror and see his ovoid face?"

Leibowitz thrust his little grey beard out, pointing it stiffly at me.

I SURRENDER MY bag to the man who's waiting for our train in Kraków, his sign bearing our misspelled names. Rolling it along behind him, with Leibowitz's bag on his shoulder, he escorts us to his car, and I watch through the window as a block-and-a-half of Kraków rolls by.

God only knows what we've paid him for this service.

Perhaps Leibowitz is right. Perhaps we *are* simply shills in an international swindle, displaced from our homes and our cities, only to have them sold back to us fifty or sixty years later as tourist attractions.

Exhausted, I stand beneath the high ceilings of my hotel room, waiting for Leibowitz to excuse himself to his own room, but he sits instead on the bed nearest the windows and begins blackening his shoes, his blunt hand stuffed inside the shoe's mouth, the other massaging a chamois across it, and I realize that it is only here, in booking a single room, that his mother's friend has spared our expenses.

"I need some air," I say, and immediately Leibowitz rises to his feet. Capping the polish and folding his chamois, he restores each to its place in his daub kit.

"I'll go with you," he says, completely dressed before I have even managed to retighten my tie, his suit this time a white linen affair made from enough material for a small circus tent, "unless you prefer going alone, of course?"

The question is little more than a rhetorical flourish, and yet, to my horror, I hear myself responding, "No, no, I'd be pleased for the company."

"You're certain, then?"

"Of course," I say, "yes," the *S* brittle and clipped against the tips of my teeth.

"Well," he purrs inside a moue, "if you insist, I'll be right out. We'll go to the Jewish Quarter, then. To Kazimierz, eh?"

He pulls the bathroom door closed behind him, leaving me in the middle of the room, listening to the faltering spill of his urine.

Despising myself and unable to bear it any longer, I grab my hat and pick up my room key from the writing desk; slipping through the door and rushing down the hallway, I pound the elevator buttons; too impatient to wait for the car, I dash down the stairs and run through the lobby into the street, losing myself happily among the thronging Poles, laughing almost maniacally, so grateful am I to be rid of him.

ON WAWEL HILL, two soldiers in antique uniforms guard the castle's mammoth doors. One cocks his rifle with a crack, scattering the schoolchildren who have been surreptitiously approaching him. A gypsy woman sits with her child on the curb of Bernardynska Street, her feet in the gutter. Crossing away from her, I end up strolling behind two policemen. They stop when they notice me behind them and look into a shop window until I pass and they can follow me.

A flyer on the door of the new Jewish Cultural Center announces a lecture on antisemitism in English for later in the evening.

I think to call Isabelle from a pay phone on the street, but can't remember if I'm eight hours ahead or behind. I don't want to wake her, neither do I feel like hearing her say "I told you so" when she asks me how the trip has been. Besides, I've yet to change my money and it feels too good wandering the streets alone, and so I promise myself I'll call her later.

Eventually, Stradomska turns into Krakowska Street and I pass a long, curving wall plastered top to bottom with a repetitive

Sony ad, each square of the ad depicting the back of the same shaved head, the head wearing the same set of earphones but a different hat in each poster: a bowler, a tasseled nightcap, a Tibetan *zhva-mo*.

Kitschy klezmer-style Muzak wafts from speakers hidden in the trees. A large sign on a building announces departure times for the SCHINDLER'S LIST TOUR. There's a gigantic menorah with two plaster Lions of Judah stationed above the entrance of a dingy restaurant, and I realize that, without intending to, I have wandered into the Jewish quarter, into Kazimierz.

Most of the buildings in its ramshackle main square have been converted into galleries and shops. I stick my head into some of these, but they hold little of interest and so I wander instead down the back roads, away from the main square into a labyrinth of narrowing streets. The high plaster walls on either side are topped with barbed wire and covered with incomprehensible graffiti. I'm considering returning to the hotel, when a thunderclap sounds and the sky begins to pour rain. Clutching my hat, I curse myself for bringing neither an umbrella nor my guidebook with its maps. I dash along, searching for shelter, striking blindly down one tangled alley after another, plunging heedlessly forward.

"Ah, fuck you, Leibowitz!" I scream, throwing my hat, ruined and sopping, into a garbage bin.

Advancing without logic or reason, my suit coat wrapped about my head, I come upon an opening, the meeting place of three alleyways, and standing at this triple crossroads, I hear the strangest thing.

"Hello?" I shout.

But there is no response.

"Hello?"

I assume I'm imagining it, that it's an aural hallucination of some kind; after all, I haven't eaten since last night. However, as I continue through the rain towards the voice—a man's, chanting, unmistakably, in Hebrew—it grows progressively louder.

"Hello?" I shout again.

And again, "Hello?"

It must be the evening service, prayed by some surviving remnant. Halina had, in fact, mentioned that at least one of Kraków's many synagogues was still functioning. With a quickening curiosity, I follow the sound as best I can to a large, yellow building, where an enormous twin staircase leads to a second-floor entrance.

A sign at the bottom reads SYNAGOGA IZAAKA.

I climb the stairs and, entering the doorway, find two young men seated behind a long table in the vestibule, both wearing shiny taffeta yarmulkes. One lifts a brochure and, nodding, offers it to me with a pale hand.

"Is there a service here?" I say.

"Prayer? A prayer service," I try again, when it's clear he doesn't understand me.

"Davening," I say, "you know?" And imitating a Jew in prayer,

I bend rapidly at the waist, although now they seem to understand me even less. I begin again. "Jews? *Yidn?* You know: *Yidn?*"

"*Yidn?*" the one says blankly to the other.

"*Yidn?*" the other replies, looking blankly back.

They speak to each other in Polish.

"*Żyd?*" I say, remembering the Polish word.

"*Żyd?*" they say.

"*Żyd, Żyd,* yes," I say, "praying, prayer," bringing my hands flat together below my chin and genuflecting slightly.

"Ah, prayer, praying," one of them says.

"Yes, praying," I say. "Jews — *Żyds* — praying?"

"No, no," the first one says, shaking his head.

"No *Żyd?*" I say, pointing with my thumb towards the sanctuary door.

"No. No *Żyd.* Loop. Is tape loop. Tape?" the other boy says, his hands moving in circles before him.

"Ah, tape, I see. A tape loop, yes."

And paying the necessary złotys anyway, I pick up my program and am about to enter the sanctuary when they call me back and offer me a shiny yarmulke similar to the ones they're wearing.

I balance mine on my own head and enter the sanctuary.

Beneath its high, molded ceilings, there are rows and rows of empty wooden pews, each with a number stenciled onto its back.

Wet and chilled, I take a seat.

Along the walls, in peeling frescoes, are the words of several Hebrew prayers. The audio loop booms out what I'm almost certain is the Yom Kippur service. A television set, on a table near the Holy Ark, broadcasts historical film clips, also on a loop. The same figures, I notice, periodically scroll across its screen.

Stationed at various points in the room are life-size black-and-white cardboard cut-outs of Jews in what must here be considered characteristic poses. A flat, two-dimensional, thickly bearded Jew wrapped in a prayer shawl holds an open prayer book in one hand, the other placed so that it seems to cling to the velvet rope sectioning off the Ark from visitor access. A cardboard Hasid stoops behind him in a long coat and a round, furry hat, a silver beard falling across his sunken chest. Near the exit, a third clasps an ancient hat in one gently curling fist and an umbrella in the other. His neatly trimmed beard covers his chin; his earlocks fall in luxuriant curls on either side of his forehead. Tucked beneath his arm, he seems to be holding a coffee grinder or perhaps an old box camera. Could the photo be a self-portrait? I wonder. Each figure is mounted on a wooden spine affixed to the black silhouette of its back.

Ruefully, I thrust my chin up and the yarmulke falls onto the floor. I gaze into the empty women's section in the upstairs balcony, and I can't help enjoying the low farce of it all: all the amenities of Jewish life without the pesky Jews. What could be better?

What is a Jew anyway, except the Red Indian of the European continent? Having successfully exterminated him, his murderers (or at least their descendents) are free to sentimentally admire his superior culture while simultaneously misrepresenting it.

If I laugh, it's a bitter laugh, and I'm reminded of the sort of jokes my sisters and I used to share when we were children. Whenever one of us went away for a week to a student council camp or even sometimes for an overnight at a friend's, the others would smuggle little handwritten notes into the suitcase of the traveler. It was a sweet jest, really. The traveler would arrive and open his bags and, as skirts or pants and shirts were folded and put away, dozens of brightly colored squares of paper fluttered out of their creases, bearing jokes, good wishes, and words of encouragement.

Invariably, among these tattered messages was the one familiar from its occasional postings on our bathroom door, where it appeared sometimes with a small drawing of a dripping faucet sketched (as if for extra reassurance) beneath its signature:

> The showers are fine.
> I have fixed the showers.
> Enjoy your stay!
> Signed,
> Adolf the Plumber

Adolf the Plumber was, of course, Adolf Hitler, escaped to the States and, cleverly if not completely disguised, still pursu-

ing his Final Solution, now on a more modest scale, one subur-
ban shower stall at a time.

I pictured him, for some reason, in blue-and-white railroad
overalls and a matching cap, his mustache, full and wiry, bristling across his entire lip, his red eyes betraying a certain anxi-
ety when he entered our house and asked to be shown to the
toilets.

Why my parents allowed their children to indulge in so dark
a humor, I have no idea. I myself would have sent Franny to a
psychiatrist at the first posting. Of course, the pathos was lost
on us at the time. We were children and we considered it an excellent, even a daring, joke. Hitler was a comic figure, not unlike Charlie Chaplin, a small man with an absurd mustache,
who occasionally appeared in the Looney Tunes cartoons I
watched every day after kindergarten, animated propaganda shorts
from the Second World War. In one, I remember the Führer, in
tears, ranting in an ersatz German after gremlins demolish his
airplane. I thought I understood the joke and, when I was five,
I raised my arm in a stiff salute, greeting my great-uncle Alfred
with a squeaky "Heil Hitler!"

"Don't say that, Charlie," he scolded me, "or they'll throw you
in jail!"

Perhaps his reaction accounts, at least in part, for the paranoia that crackled like the background radiation of some form-
ative Big Bang, haunting me as a child. Or perhaps it wasn't
paranoia at all. In my second-grade class, for example, at Doddling

Elementary School in Karkel, Texas, whenever my teacher, Mrs. McGoin, mentioned anything having to do with either Jews or Judaism—if she said the word *draydl,* for instance, or *matzahs* or *Passover*—the entire class of twenty-eight children would unfailingly turn, as a single body, and stare at me.

It was an unnerving experience: twenty-eight little heads rotating and staring and rotating back.

Is it any wonder that later I used to sit in our synagogue in Karkel, thinking to myself, "Isn't it naïve, a little naïve of us, to gather here together punctually each week as a community at the same time and in the same place with our telltale symbols displayed across the outside of our building, so that even an inattentive terrorist might know exactly where to find us?"

"*Aha!* I thought I'd find you here!" Leibowitz digs his nails into my arm. "You found the Quarter. Good, good, excellent, good: *tsevishen yidn vert men nit farfalen,* eh?"

He pulls me up from my pew and drags me back into the street, elevating his umbrella above our heads and sheltering us both beneath it.

Forcing his arm through mine, he grapples me close to him and mewls, "I do so apologize. I hadn't realized how very long I was taking, Belski. It must have been that wretched airplane food! Grim, a grim meal, and I may even have fallen asleep. In any case, I didn't hear you knocking, although you were correct, quite correct, to leave without me when I didn't respond. I would have done the same in your stead, believe me, exactly the same."

His face, too near mine, leers malevolently and his breath is vinegary, as though he had only recently been eating pickled herring.

"Ah," he says, "but here we are again, together at last!"

Heading us towards the main square, he wanders the streets like a manic flâneur, taking in everything, compulsively a-jiggle with conversational observations, his expansive body pummeling into my frailer flesh, squeezing into me, pinioning me against various city walls, whenever he wishes to make a point. It's a bit like strolling with a marionette whose puppeteer has prepared for the performance by ingesting a large dosage of amphetamine.

Finally we stop in the main square, in front of a toy shop housed in what used to be the *mikveh*.

"Ah! Now, let me see." Leibowitz squints into the gloom. "Where are those restaurants again?"

miniature hasidic men in tiny fur streimels

There are two so-called Jewish restaurants next door to each other in Kazimierz, both inexplicably named Ariel, and each owned not by Jews but by feuding Polish brothers.

The White Ariel, in the building with the iron menorah and the two Lions of Judah, seems, for all its kitsch, less forbidding than its neighbor, the Green Ariel, which resembles a downscale pub.

But of course, it's into the Green Ariel that Leibowitz commandeers me. We stand in its foyer, waiting to be seated, while our eyes adjust to its dark interior. The cash register is lined with little trinkets for sale, miniature statues of Hasidic men in tiny fur *streimels*, their little beards glued onto their chins, their chintzy prayer shawls, each draped like the scarf of an aviatrix around their wooden necks. Fat in full skirts, heads covered in miniature babuskas, the tiny women figurines hold Shabbos candlesticks made of toothpicks, one in each carved hand, the tips painted red and yellow, suggesting flame.

A tape by the Klezmatics squalls over the sound system.

"Welcome home, Reb Belski! Welcome home!" Leibowitz hisses into my ear. Gripping my arm, he ushers me into the restaurant, and we follow our waiter to a table in a corner of the room.

FOR REASONS THAT remain obscure to me, I know several otherwise cultured men who eat with their mouths open, and Leibowitz, of course, is one of these. I'm compelled to watch as pickles slather across his tongue and knishes turn to mush between his teeth. He speaks incessantly, pausing only to gnaw at a lamb bone or to lick at his thumb, the long, curving nail of which is coated with sauces and creams. Bits of kielbasa, flying propulsively from his mouth, entangle in his beard or land on the serving platters we are sharing. Each time a particle of pickled egg or stewed cabbage or jellied carp hits one of our common platters, I mentally catalogue it as forbidden to me.

Eventually, however, all the platters are catalogued as forbidden and even my own plate becomes too defiled to eat from. In a defensive move, I place my hand casually over the mouth of my beer glass, lest I be deprived of its alcoholic succor.

Because he eats so voraciously and speaks so relentlessly, Leibowitz can't help choking periodically. Turning to the side, he heaves out throat-rattling coughs that sound as though they are stripping the lining from his esophagus. His belly heaves and trembles, and more foods fly about in these pantophagistic eruptions. His tie and the lapels of his once immaculate linen jacket become mottled with stains.

Like a priest offering a benediction, he raises his hand, his index finger lifted, his napkin clutched between its palm and three fingers, signaling me that he will speak again as soon as he has sipped from his water. Eyes bleary, he attempts to regain his composure.

"Are you ready?" he says, his voice scratchy from the seizure.

I confess I have no idea what he's talking about and the frank, almost sexual undertone of his advance makes me slightly nervous.

"Belski, how long are we going to dance around this thing? We're grown men, after all.

"Oh, but you're such a rascal!" he says. "No, you really are. Aren't you in the least curious? Now that we're here together and finally alone."

I open my mouth, but the ability to speak has ebbed from me completely.

"Ah, so shy, my dear shy boy," he says, and then a bit more sternly, "Now, I listened to *your* paper and so I thought I'd lay out mine. As a sort of dress rehearsal, you understand. Before the conference. Get your impression in time to make any important changes. Of course, I wouldn't want to impose. . . ." His face becomes an obscene leer of resentment.

"No, no," I stammer. "I'd be honored," I say.

"Honored? Really?" he says, and again, "Really?"

"Really," I say.

"Well, it *is* a fascinating thesis," he says, and he's off, literally for the next three hours, during which time I signal periodically to the waiter for another beer and then another and then for a vodka and finally for a long series of aperitifs.

"You recall, do you not, Belski, that I asked you some time ago to send me copies of antisemitic caricatures of Gustav Mahler?"

These drawings ran in various Viennese newspapers accompanying articles decrying Mahler as an "unadulterated Jew" whose "Jew-boy antics" on the conductor's podium were an outrage to Viennese society.

"Well, I noticed a remarkable thing." Leibowitz leans in towards me. "Not that these drawings are remarkable. They're not. In their range of visual representation, they are, indeed, typical of antisemitic drawings for their time.

"The parodic imagination, Belski, is, by its own intention and design, quite limited in means, referring only to a preconceived notion of type shared equally by the caricaturist and his audience. Now, *that* is fundamental and clear. There must be a shared currency of features, a common vocabulary, as it were, a catalogue of easily recognizable and stereotypic traits, for these drawings to have their intended impact. Otherwise, one would simply look at such a picture and say, 'Well, that doesn't quite resemble Mahler, does it?' "

In Vienna, for a Jew, these features meant a hooked nose, protuberant lips, a rounded head, a curved spine, a bent back, and a salacious leer.

"Now, in these drawings that you sent me, one can see these stock traits merging with the lines of Mahler's actual face and form, his manner of dress, his habit of stance. His nose becomes hooked and enlarged. His eyes, behind his rimless glasses, develop a lascivious squint. The head is made overlarge, even for Mahler, whose head, as you know, was in fact quite large. The feet are splayed; the hands become apish, twitching monstrosities. He becomes, in fact, the exemplar of the 'mongrel race' Jews were thought by some Europeans to be, most infamously by Houston Stewart Chamberlain, Wagner's son-in-law, no less, who maintained, not as a private opinion, but in his published writings, that Jews had 'hybridized'—that is his term, Belski— 'hybridized' with Africans during the Alexandrian exile, their bodies, as a result, becoming the crude mishmash of parts he so pseudo-scientifically perceived them to be."

Leibowitz breaks off for a long excursus upon the life and work of Houston Stewart Chamberlain and also upon the history and misuses of phrenology, to which he claims to be a "sometimes skeptical adherent," his own cranium size, tabulated phrenologically with genius—"Goethe, Napoleon, Jefferson, all had tiny skulls. Examine their death masks, if you don't believe me."—eventually returning to the topic at hand: "Perhaps it was the late hour, perhaps the Benedictine, perhaps merely the goddess of inspiration lighting on my fevered brow, but in poring over these crude if, in some cases, quite artistically rendered drawings, I was struck one evening by the extent to which Mahler, our own dear Gustav, resembled in them the shape and form of one Julius Henry Marx, more famously known to us all as . . . Groucho!"

Dramatically, he bites off a piece of chrust.

"I know what you're thinking," he says, spewing out a blunderbuss of moistened crumbs. "Ridiculous!" he says, bringing his hand, too late, to his mouth. "I know, I know," he chews hurriedly, "and yet . . . and yet, consider: the rounded glasses, the disheveled hair, the lengthy nose, the leering eye, the crooked broken-backed stance, even the ridiculous swallowtail conductor's jacket: Groucho couldn't have resembled these caricatures of Mahler more had he in fact modeled himself on them. Ah, but you've never noticed this?

"Of course not," he says. "But I did, you see!

"And you're correct, of course, that while it strains credulity to believe that Groucho actually or intentionally modeled his costume on these parodies, it is *not* far-fetched to believe that he astutely drew upon the same repertoire of crude tropes that the Viennese caricaturists employed, costuming himself, quite intentionally, as an antisemite's parody of a Jew.

"A meta-parody! A parody of a parody, as it were!"

As Leibowitz leans forward, the tip of his beard grazes the top of his interlaced fists. He closes his eyes and begins to croon the chorus of the song playing over the PA:

> *Zol shoyn kumen di geule,*
> *Zol shoyn kumen di geule,*
> *Zol shoyn kumen di geule,*
> *Meshiekh kumt shoyn bald.*

His little head, in fact, seems to be dancing among the platters of potato knish and coleslaw as he repeats the chorus, his beard dipping like a basting brush into the mustard sauce.

It's a grotesque and strange vision, and one from which I doubt I'll fully recover, I think, as he sits back and fixes me with a hard, mad glare.

"I began with new eyes—with new eyes, Belski!—to examine photos of all the Marxes—not only Groucho, no, no, but also Harpo, Chico, and even Zeppo as well—and to review their films—which are a delight, an utter delight. And I can tell you that, analyzed carefully, the four brothers seem to form a sort of Ascent-of-Man spectrum of European Jewish stereotypes on the path towards assimilation."

As though we were conspirators, he whispers this, glancing

nervously at the Poles who, in groups of twos and threes and fours, sit like waiting sharks around the little island of our table. They smoke their cigarettes and laugh into their beers, paying no attention to us.

Leibowitz says, "Now of course, you've seen those models of Darwinian theory, the figures proceeding from left to right, starting with an ape-like primate and moving along through Homo erectus to Homo neanderthal to Homo sapiens to modern man, yes?"

Completely drunk, I assure him that I know exactly what he is talking about.

"Well, my model of the Ascent of Assimilating Jewish Man begins with Harpo on the extreme left—Harpo, you know? The one who played the harp? The mute one? With the baggy coat and the red, curly hair, the red fright wig? which, incidentally, is not at all unlike the wig worn traditionally by actors playing Barabas, Belski—Barabas, yes!—the gleefully murderous Jew in Marlow's *Jew of Malta*. And you will surely recall that Olivier wore just such a red fright wig to play his famous Shylock.

"Now, if this is a coincidence, then it is a striking coincidence. But soft. Let us consider Harpo as the archetypal *luftmensch*, a familiar shtetl figure, a man living seemingly on air, an air-man: a *luftmensch*. And why not, eh? Harpo's garb *is* slightly Hasidic, is it not? The long, baggy coat, the formal hat, which, I might point out, as though in deference to Jewish custom, he never removes. Slightly magical, he's frightening in a nearly sinister way; a devil able to produce steaming cups of coffee from the inside pockets of his baggy caftan, he is, like the Jew of Europe, the ultimate alien. No one knows where he's from, except that it's Absolute Elsewhere.

"And—most importantly!—like the Jew of Europe, the mute Harpo is denied a language of his own and must fashion one for himself out of the spare parts of other languages, a fragmentary pidgin sampled from barbaric yawps and horn bleats. And isn't that exactly what Yiddish sounded like, not only to the cultivated German ear, but even to the ears of your cultivated, assimilating Jews, your Herzls and your Freuds, Belski, who, turning their embarrassed backs upon their Eastern brethren, wouldn't have been caught dead haggling or kvetching in Yiddish?"

Practically fawning over himself, so pleased is he with his theory, Leibowitz directs my attention a step further to the right on his model.

"To Chico, the pianist, an Italian supposedly, in a too small jacket and a little conical hat like Pinocchio's. Now, this is important, Belski. Pay attention here. The waiter will bring your drink when it's ready. Are you listening to me? Listen to me!

"Now. In his attempt to assimilate into the dominant culture, unlike Harpo, Chico has acquired a language, although it's a mixed tongue, corrupted by accent and foreign intonation, of course, neither quite English nor Italian. And the fact that he chooses this absurd Italian, rather than an equally absurd Yid-

dish *mauscheln,* is a further—and, I might add, masterful—
tweaking of the antisemitic stereotypes.

"But let me explain what I mean."

Gnawing at the earpiece of his glasses, Leibowitz leans back
and stares at the ceiling beams, as though inspiration were con-
cealed amid its air-conditioning shafts.

"Consider for a moment the stock characters who surround
the Marx Brothers in each of their films, Belski, those lifeless
Hollywooden B and sometimes even C players, stiffly posed and
humorless. Now, they know that Chico is not, and can never become, one of them. Even were he not hobbled by his ridiculous
garments, his inability to speak as they do would forever keep
him out of their society.

"For the audience, however—and this is the crucial thing—
the stock players are indistinguishably boring and unmemorably
the same. Our sympathies are not with them, but rather with the
Brothers themselves. And in this way—ah! ah! you're ahead of
me here, I see—yes, in this way— *exactly,* Belski—the audience
becomes ethnically implicated, Judaicized, as it were, for while
Chico the character may be unaware of the ridiculous subaltern
figure he cuts, Chico the performer is in absolute control of the
portrayal: wheeling and dealing over scraps and pittances in last
season's castoffs, mangling the English tongue, he *consciously*
presents himself as absurdly marginalized. And here, look closely!
The astute viewer understands that Chico's pseudo-Italian persona
is not only a conscious mask which conceals and simultaneously

reveals his Jewishness, it's also a sly confirmation of the anti-semite's mistrust of the beguiling, nefarious Jew—for not only does the Jew speak in codes, but *here* he even speaks in codes about the codes in which he speaks."

Leibowitz raises his finger to emphasize his point, its tip encrusted with a now-dry cream sauce.

"This is a subtle point and one which your Wagner never properly understood. My God! Look at all those shabby, insulting Jewlike caricatures in his operas—the tricky Mime in *Siegfried,* the poseur Beckmesser in *Die Meistersinger,* the greedy dwarf Alberich in *Das Rheingold*—all of them and each of them a spiteful travesty, an anti-Jewish caricature delivered to their audience in a spiteful anti-Jewish code, familiar to them from the satirical cartoons that ran each and every day in their newspapers, whereas Jews, on the other hand, Belski—Jews, and the Marx Brothers specifically—use these caricatures, taking them on fully, as a way of implicating and condemning not only themselves as Jews, but *also* their antisemitic tormenters as well.

"'I am the one and only living Mime,' your beloved Mahler wrote to his stage designer, Roller. 'You wouldn't believe what there is in that part, nor what I could make of it.' A self-erasing Jew, an economic convert to Catholicism—they wouldn't allow him to conduct on the Viennese stage otherwise—Mahler understood this phenomenon only too well.

"You see, the conflicted Jew presents to the world a false face that is recognized as false by his fellow Jews in a way that is different from how it is seen as false by non-Jews. By that, I mean, whereas the non-Jew believes that Chico's character is a parody of an Italian, the Jew in the audience, understanding the codes, understands it as a caricature of a Jew.

"Why, the films themselves are playfully aware of this tension. 'Hey, since when did you become an opera singer?' Chico asks another scheming immigrant in *A Night at the Opera*. 'Since when did you become an Italian?' he is promptly answered back."

Reaching across the table, Leibowitz pours himself a large vodka.

Hoping for a check, I search for the waiter, a big Slavic-faced man with a dirty rag hung over his shoulder, but he is nowhere in sight.

"Where were we?" Leibowitz says, smacking his tongue against his soft palate. "Oh yes: Groucho!"

According to Leibowitz, with Groucho, another step to the right on his model, Assimilating Jewish Man finally obtains a fluent English, something neither Harpo nor Chico achieved.

"Indeed, in a quite stereotypically Jewish move, not only does Groucho master the master's tongue, but he wields it now with razor-sharp precision, as though it were a whip studded with multilingual puns and foreign phrases, insinuating double entendres and sly innuendos, quite beyond the abilities of the tongue-tied stock players whose stilted dialogue, as I've said, is forever dull and bland.

"No, in Groucho's hand, English is a weapon wielded against every person he encounters, principally and most conspicuously against himself: 'I would never join a club that would have me as a member,' he says, famously lacerating himself with this whip, in one stroke restricting himself from his enemies' finest tables. Told, in real life, at a Beverly Hills country club, that he couldn't use the pool, he quipped, 'Well, since my daughter is only half-Jewish, can she go in up to her knees?'

"Compare his rapid gestures to the formal poses struck by the stock players—his herky-jerky gait to their stiff struts; his leering, id-ridden libido to the studiously naïve sexual decorum of the dowagers he attempts to seduce, for their money, of course; his flat intonations to the others' stagy pronunciations—and you have a perfect late-century catalogue of European antisemitic tropes.

"And, as a side note, Belski, if I may be permitted to digress for a moment, one may compare Groucho's ludicrous tuxedo to the equally ludicrous formal wear worn by the young and completely assimilated Jews who comprised the first Zionist Congress in Basel. The image of these young, fresh-faced *yidn*, dressed up in formal suits and gowns for an evening of mixed dancing, desperately trying to be modern and European, meanwhile turning their backs on European modernity in order to return to their ancient homeland, contains everything you know and need to know about the State of Israel—ah! aha!—but that is another meal altogether!"

He rubs his hands gleefully. "Perhaps at lunch, after our trip to Auschwitz tomorrow, we can discuss it in full.

"Now, where was I? Ah yes. Groucho, Groucho, wherefore art thou Groucho!

"Observe. Now, although, unlike his brothers, Groucho has assimilated into the dominant society, even into positions of power within it—he is, after all, the President of Fredonia in *Duck Soup;* you may think of Henry Kissinger here—he is never fully trusted, nor is he fully trustworthy.

"His mustache, that suave signifier of fin de siècle gentility, is the tip-off. Why, it's as fake as his long Jewish nose is real! And significantly, though he may resist them for the first four reels of each film, by the fifth reel, Groucho inevitably rejoins his raggedy brothers Harpo and Chico, sliding down the social ladder, back inside the ghetto walls, where he is finally more comfortable and more completely himself.

"The famous scene from *Duck Soup* in which he cannot distinguish his own reflection from the masquerade his brothers, disguised as him, throw into his face, with nightgowns and nightcaps and greasepaint mustaches of their own, speaks volumes here. Volumes!"

Folding his arms across his belly, Leibowitz suddenly leans back in his chair and, just as suddenly, sits forward, dropping his head wearily into his hands. His elbows propped against the table, he groans, "Oy, who needs goyim, Belski, who needs goyim, when we ourselves are masters of antisemitism? A real Jew would be overwhelmed to the point of nausea, faced with this parade of dehumanizing stereotypes, these images stolen from our enemies' sketchbooks and turned against ourselves. But we, who are so far from our radiant, original selves, can only laugh. And indeed, why not laugh, for what is Jewish life now except a comic interlude between two towering tragedies, the one historical and ineluctable, the other unknown but no less avoidable?"

"And what about Zeppo?"

"Em?" he says, looking up at me.

I'm finally drunk enough to challenge him.

"Isn't Zeppo a hole in your theory?" I say, as the waiter brings us our bill of eighty-five zlotys, much more than I'd anticipated.

"Ah yes! yes! Very good. Very good, Belski!" Leibowitz, bright again, snatches up the cheque. "That is indeed the $613,000 question! What about Zeppo indeed!"

He looks at me as though I were the smartest and most devoted of his pupils.

"Zeppo is what makes this all so very fascinating," he says. "Zeppo, the comedy act's straight man, is, of course, on the extreme right of our Ascent of Assimilating Man. Wearing no costume other than an ordinary suit, without wig or hat or makeup of any kind, indeed having no comic persona of his own, resembling, in fact, the stock players more than he does his own brothers so that an uninformed child watching any of the five films in which he appears before his early retirement from the act in 1935 would not be able to pick him out as one of the Marxes, Zeppo is so assimilated that ultimately, like most Jews, Belski—well, like you yourself, for instance, with your blonde shiksa wife and your goyishe daughter—he eventually leaves the act altogether!"

At that moment, feeling horribly alone, I realize I've neglected to call Isabelle.

"Let's split this down the middle, shall we?" Leibowitz scowls, frowning farsightedly at the bill. "It's easier that way, don't you think?"

WE UNDRESS IN the near-dark. Leibowitz leaves the bathroom door open slightly, allowing a crack of light to spill into the room. Having insisted upon keeping the windows open as well, he chooses for himself the bed farthest from their draughts.

I don't have the strength to argue with him and, instead, turn away from the light and place my head upon my pillow, only to find myself staring into the eyes of the Madonna frescoed onto the wall of the church opposite our hotel. Barefoot on a crescent moon, she clasps three bloody arrows in each of her raised fists, and she seems to stare at me in an angry, accusing way.

I can't sleep. The lights and the roulade of city sounds from the street are the least of it. Beneath the huffing and puffing of Leibowitz's apnea, a simple declarative sentence pounds in my brain:

ppo. I am Zeppo. I am Zeppo. I am Zeppo. I am Zeppo. I am Zep

And instantly I recognize the thought as true. I am Zeppo. I am Zeppo. I *am* Zeppo, blandly assimilated, physically stiff and awkward, dressing British and thinking my thoughts in a banal English.

Turning over, I watch Leibowitz's mammoth paunch rising and falling beneath his covers, silhouetted against the bathroom light. If you shouted into his ear in Yiddish that the hotel is on fire, he'd rush for the windows, while I, sitting in the midst of flames, would have to ask for clarification, because I am Zeppo. I am Zeppo. I *am* Zeppo, father and potential grandfather of goyim, an endless river of Gentile descendents who, due to the Talmudic laws of matrilineal descent, will wander the earth distinct from me in essence, taking communion, perhaps, or worse, being baptized in rivers, sleeping beneath idolatrous crucifixes, comforted by all manner of contradictory theologies, meditating in zendos or praying dhikr in mosques, oppressing the Jews of their community when, as the Passover Haggadah tells us, at least once in every generation, the opportunity arises, while I, long dead, am called to the celestial Torah in the Prayer House of the Supernal Heavens by my rightful name: Zeppo ben Yitzhak ben Yehezkiel ben Chaim HaLevi!

Every hour on the hour, a trumpeter in the Mariacki Church

tower plays a mournful tune to the four directions, the notes collapsing at a specified measure in a strangled sound, as though someone had scored the throttling of a goose.

(According to local legend, during a Tartar invasion, it was precisely at this point in his alarums that the original trumpeter's throat was pierced by an arrow and, for some reason, the city fathers of Kraków thought to incorporate this garroted glissando into the hourly chiming of their city's clock.)

Certainly, the only thing worse than hearing this charivari at two in the morning is hearing it again at three and at four, the notes, in their pained descent, collapsing into silence every hour on the hour, and in my half-drowsing state, I begin to imagine the passage refers specifically to me.

In a feverish dream, I see myself as Zeppo Marx, high on an ancient parapet, defending Jerusalem from an advancing horde of Nibelungen led by Mahler and Wagner, with Wagner's wife, Cosima (or is it Isabelle? I can't tell: the two are somehow twinned), trailing behind in a light carriage, transcribing into Wagner's diary a description of the battle, including a small footnote concerning my death as an arrow pierces my throat and I topple from my tower, unprotected by costume or armor, plummeting in a stupid seersucker suit and a white straw hat, unrecognized even by my brothers Harpo, Chico and Groucho, at whose sandaled feet I land.

At the moment of my death, I'm awakened by a feral-like scratching at the door.

"Leibowitz!" I whisper, immediately awake.

"There's someone at the door!" I shout quietly, unable to rouse him.

"They've come!" I whisper.

"Get the door!" I hiss, but he continues sleeping soundly as the scratching grows louder.

Not knowing what to do, I leave my bed, gliding along the floor in my stocking feet. There is no peephole and so, instead (stupidly, I know, I know) I open the door and the room is immediately flooded with intense light from the brightly lit hallway.

A man with a shaved head is there, bending on one knee, balancing while attempting to place a small advertisement inside the crack between our door and its frame. He looks up at me, his blue eyes blinking, helplessly astonished, behind unusually thick eyeglasses. We stare at one another for a long, silent moment, as though each of us is uncertain who was dream and who dreamer.

"Sorry. Oh, oh, so sorry!" he says in a crisp and reassuring British accent. "Have I awakened you? Dreadful, dreadful," he says. And "Here," he says, handing me the ad he's been working so furiously to place inside our door, a small, rectangular strip with a phone number on it and a grainy black-and-white photograph of a nude woman leaning back in a pornographic yoga pose, her legs folded beneath her knees, her breasts rising into the air.

this dour pilgrimage or, zeppo in auschwitz

Leibowitz's cologne is particularly vile this morning, and in an attempt to evade it, I press myself against the car door, edging as near to the window as I can. The streets of Kraków, clotted with cars and trucks, however, are equally rife with diesel fumes.

Our guide for the day is a tall, elegant man named Kryztof. His grey pompadour is swept dashingly off his forehead; his handsome face hangs like an ironically interested moon between his seat back and the driver's. As the Mercedes snakes through traffic, he wryly points out attractive women on the street as though they were a part of our tour.

"Well, *you* two certainly do have a lot in common!" Leibowitz sputters through the little black hole in his beard.

"What?" I say.

"Why do people always say 'what?' when they've obviously heard whatever's just been said?" he asks me peevishly.

"What?" I say.

"There! Now you've done it again. Ach, it's a curious phenomenon—this asking of 'what?' when you've obviously just heard what I've just said, didn't you? Or didn't you?"

I admit to him that I actually had.

"Yes, and people do this all the time. Oh, and it's just so tedious, all these extra steps thrown in to sabotage a simple conversation."

I turn a sympathetic face towards Kryztof in the hope of indicating to him, through gesture and mien, that I understand what a difficult customer Leibowitz can be, simultaneously disassociating myself from Leibowitz while attempting to ameliorate the experience for the Poles, at least to a minor degree.

My efforts are insufficient, however, against the onslaught of Leibowitz's corrosive personality and his mood, which for some reason is even more horrible this morning.

We've barely left the city limits when he leans forward, straining against his seat belt, and begins peppering Kryztof with questions about Polish antisemitism and Poland's complicity with the Nazis during the war. Citing a long list of atrocities and massacres, he's as blunt as a drunk at a cockfight.

Kryztof, smiling stiffly, attempts to counter these accusations in a patient tone. Christian Poles were not opportunistically antisemitic (this is Leibowitz's snarling phrase); they were, in fact, Hitler's first victims, murdered alongside the Jewish Poles, whose number (three million) he counts among Poland's six million civilian wartime dead.

Not for nothing is Poland called the Christ of Nations, he reminds us.

"Why, Janusz's own father"—he indicates our driver with an elegant nod of his head—"was a fighter in the Polish underground —isn't that right, Janusz?—and was killed at Auschwitz."

"*Tak.* I was eleven when war ended," Janusz says. "We were to Auschwitz, to look, to see, but . . ."

He shrugs, lifting both hands for a moment from the wheel, and I'm shocked, as though with a jolt of electricity, to see that he is missing three fingers from his left hand.

"*Tatuś* fell off a guard tower, did he?" Leibowitz guffaws in a theatrical aside.

Kryztof shifts in his seat. He scans the landscape outside the car's windows. His gracefully sculpted nostrils flare almost imperceptibly, and he sighs.

"Of course, there is still antisemitism in Poland," he says, grimacing, "but today, Poland's antisemites hate all other ethnic groups, as well."

"Ah, well, so, there's been progress," Leibowitz says.

"Yes, of course there has," Kryztof says, glancing at his watch.

We arrive at Auschwitz shortly after eleven. Apparently, the screening of the preparatory film has already begun.

"I am sorry, but now, we will have to run," Kryztof says.

"Hurry. Hurry, please!" he calls to me, motioning from a distance with his long, graceful arms, as he and Leibowitz, having dashed from the car, gallop across the parking lot and disappear into the museum's entrance.

I follow at a slower pace, losing them inside the twists and turns of the building's long corridors, unable to hurry, too conscious of the irony that I'm being forced to run through Auschwitz by a Pole barking orders at me. Disoriented, I've even begun to panic when, without warning, a door in a wall opens and Kryztof sticks his angular head through it, beckoning me into the darkened theater, where we stand at the back with others who were unable to find a seat.

I have no idea where Leibowitz is, but he's nearby, I know. His cologne hangs, like a miasma, in the air.

Watching the film between the heads of the people in front of me, I recognize many of its images from the film loop I saw at the Synagoga Izaaka yesterday: images of a drayman pulling a cart, of a woman carrying laundry, of religious men standing in a group on the street in long coats and black hats, one of them raising his palm against the camera, blocking his face in an effort not to be made into a graven image, all dissolve into the too familiar pictures of skeletal corpses stacked like cords of wood or disintegrating as ash inside the doors of an open oven.

I find myself resisting the film, its soundtrack especially, which is maudlin, its violins and horns meant to intensify images that have been seen so often now, and over so many years, that they barely retain their initial power to either shock or disturb.

All of Auschwitz is like this, I find, its reality dwarfed by some strange calculus, in comparison to the photos I've been shown of it my entire life. Being here feels mildly redundant or, worse, fetishistic, as when, for instance, neither Leibowitz nor I, marched into the open air by Kryztof, take out our cameras at the ARBEIT MACHT FREI sign at the camp's main gate.

Gesturing towards it as though it were the entrance to Nebuchadnezzar's Hanging Gardens of Babylon, and puzzled by our indifference to it, Kryztof asks, "But don't you want to take a photo?" With his chest puffed out and his arms behind his back and an insinuating leer distorting his face, he resembles a man selling pornography.

The snapshot seems unnecessary to me. Who hasn't seen the ARBEIT MACHT FREI sign? Who hasn't had its cruel ironies inked into his consciousness like a small blue tattoo? Who really needs a souvenir copy of his own?

And yet—"Like good Jews," Leibowitz chortles—we comply without resistance, taking our cameras out and posing, the three of us, in various groupings, like members of a small square dance team: Leibowitz and Kryztof; Kryztof and myself; myself and Leibowitz; then all of us together, grinning or grim-faced, arms around each other or not, while a stranger, balancing our cameras against her own, dangles the others from their straps around her wrists.

Perhaps, I can't help thinking, these photos will one day be blown up into life-size cardboard cut-outs and stationed here by the Polish Ministry of Tourism as an example of late twentieth century post-Holocaust American Jewry.

In the shuffling of the cameras, a trace of Leibowitz's cologne is transferred to my hand, and for the rest of the day, whenever I rub my nose or scratch my chin, the smell of it momentarily nauseates me.

WE ENTER THROUGH the main gate, passing a small gift kiosk stationed in an old guard house. Displayed in its windows are two sets of postcards for sale, each with photographs from the camp grounds: the gas chambers, the barbed wire fences, the guard towers, the railroad tracks, a death's head spray-painted onto a wooden wall with the words *Halt!* and *Stoj!* written below it.

"Imagine receiving one of these in the mail, eh?" Leibowitz cackles into my ear. " 'Dear Mother, Dear Father, Dear Rabbi, having a wonderful time, wish you were here!' "

Although I assume his quipping and his political caviling may be an emotional defense against the extraordinary brutality represented here, still it's fatiguing and I find myself consistently edging away from him, slipping like an errant moon from his orbit, towards Kryztof, in the hope of somehow salvaging at least a part of the experience for myself.

Kryztof, however, has long since lost patience with us both. He brushes off most of my questions, hustling us from one room of the museum to the next, seemingly making no distinction between Leibowitz and me, lumping me in with him as equally difficult and annoying, in every respect his twin, as though we were no more than two representative and interchangeable Jews come to have a peek into the violent womb that has vomited us into the modern era.

And because most of the exhibit is in Polish, much of it remains incomprehensible, Kryztof deigning to translate the commentaries only summarily and occasionally. Stationing himself at the door of each room, he allows us to prowl blindly through them on our own, referring constantly to his watch, as though he had a more engaging appointment scheduled for later in the day.

Despite this, Leibowitz dawdles and complains.

"Oh, but Adorno got it all wrong, all horribly wrong!" he exclaims too loudly as we stand with a crowd before a series of drawings, by a camp inmate, depicting guards and their captives, the captives wraithlike in black-and-white pajamas, the guards big with enormous chests, their strong teeth glinting inside clenched smirks. "Tsk-tsk-tsk," he tsks. "I'm afraid the equation is not 'No art after Auschwitz,' rather 'No *bad* art after Auschwitz!' No kitsch, if you please!"

Although I move away from him, in a way I share his detachment. Even here, the actual exhibits—the mountains of human hair, the alps of shoes and eyeglasses, the long dunes of luggage —all seem less powerful and disturbing than their familiar photographs.

Despite myself, I find that questions of aesthetics intrude. I wonder about the staff who put these exhibits together. Who, for instance, decided how much human hair or how many shoes or how many valises or how many pairs of eyeglasses are required to represent the total in a sufficiently shocking manner?

And what are these totals?

And where are the unexhibited items stored?

For instance: Does one cracked porcelain doll inside a glass exhibition table really convey what, for a million children, must have been the horror of the camps, and if not, then how many cracked porcelain dolls are necessary for that?

LIKE A SCHOOLMASTER tired of his charges, Kryztof hurries us through the crematoria and the underground interrogation cells, past the execution wall with the official Auschwitz flag flying above it, past the controversial twenty-foot-tall cross commemorating a speech the Pope gave here, stopping, only too happily, to translate the graffiti scrawled across its base.

"Strength to the Cross!" "The Cross is ours!" "Jews have nothing to do with this!" he reads through his sunglasses, before hustling us past pavilions intended for the tourists of other nations, into an old barracks set up as "a museum of martyrology," he says, "exclusively for the Jews."

It takes a moment for my eyes to adjust inside the darkened room, and when they do, I see that its black-painted walls are covered top to bottom with hundreds, perhaps even thousands, of photographs, one horrific scene after another, most of which I've never seen before.

Too grotesque to contemplate individually, the various photographs seem to assault one brutally from all sides in clusters. I stand alone in the middle of the room, my gaze whirring past them at a dizzying rate, unwilling to focus on any single image while feeling myself incapable of turning away from any one of them (lest I miss a face bearing a strong family resemblance).

I experience a nearly suffocating sense of not wishing to be here, of not needing to be here, of not wanting to be defined by this place.

As though he were reading my mind, Leibowitz is suddenly humming at my ear: "Couldn't they have contrived a more tasteful way to emotionally devastate us, emmm?" he mewls.

Before I can even think of a response, he is pulled away by an impatient Kryztof, who wants to show him a document, framed and hung on the wall, indicating that the U.S. government knew all about the camps and did nothing to stop their operations.

I can only curse Leibowitz for dragging me along with him here, implicating me into this ridiculously Jewish project of identifying oneself with the suffering imposed by others upon one's ancestors.

I can't help thinking: The graffiti at the Cross are right! Jews have absolutely nothing to do with any of this. We were merely its victims, after all. Auschwitz and the interlocking events known collectively as the Holocaust have no more to do with us than, say, the Ford Motor Plant has to do with someone whose relatives were run down en masse by a thundering fleet of Model Ts.

Why protest the Church's housing its nunneries on this bloody ground when the entire foundation of Christianity is built upon the blood of Jewish martyrs?

As for me, I will protest no more!

Let the Europeans have their bloody continent! Let the fucking Poles keep their precious Poland! Let Europe claim the Holocaust it made as its own!

I don't want it anymore!

Unable to breathe, I rush from the exhibit room into an antechamber, where a mournful voice on a tape loop intones *Av HaRachamim,* the prayer recited on behalf of those who have been martyred as Jews.

an evening of chopin

Upon discovering that we are musicologists, Kryztof suggests an evening of Chopin. He gives us two coupons for ten percent off the concert ticket price and bids us adieu on a corner of the Rynek Główny, whispering that we should offer Janusz a tip, and so we do.

Leibowitz ceremonially removes a bottle of vodka from his briefcase and hands it to Kryztof as a token of our thanks. Mumbling his own chagrined thanks, Kryztof appears discomfited by the gift, as though he were a Negro to whom Leibowitz has just presented a watermelon.

"Perhaps one day," Kryztof says, lowering his head reverently, "in ten or—who knows?—twenty years when your children come, as they must, to visit Kraków, perhaps there will be a real Jewish quarter here once again to show them."

"I should prefer that no Jew ever approach Eastern Europe again!" Leibowitz mutters, as the Mercedes roars off, leaving us in a cloud of exhaust. "May it be banned. Sacral in its negativity. Accursed!

"Still"—he grins—"a profitable morning, all in all, don't you think? At least as far as the Wagner is concerned."

It's quite hot out, and I'm not feeling well. Imagining it will be cool and dark there, I mention to Leibowitz that I might sit for a while inside a nearby cinema, hoping he will return to the hotel without me. Our train leaves early in the morning and he will need to begin packing his numerous belongings. In truth, I simply want an hour alone, but, to my dismay, Leibowitz insists upon accompanying me, as though I were a fragile child who required his overseeing.

"I really think I should come, Belski. You look horrible, just awful, terrible, in fact."

There's no dissuading him, and so the two of us wend our way down the street to the cinema I'd noticed on my walk the day before. The entrance is at street level, the box office upstairs, and as I take each step, I realize that my legs are trembling. We purchase our tickets and, not even knowing what film is playing and not really caring, I push my way into the darkened cinema.

It's hot and stuffy inside. There is apparently no air-conditioning, and although the film has already started, the picture on the screen is quite dim. I have to grope blindly forward, feeling my way by the backs of the chairs, with Leibowitz bumping continually into me, his belly pummeling my back.

"Feeling any better, old chum? Hmmm?" he hums, as soon as we have taken our seats, leaning in so near to me that the bristles of his beard brush my cheek and the brim of his straw hat scrapes my forehead.

The screen brightens with a scene change and I see that, for all our tentativeness, we could have sat almost anywhere. Except for a few old men with caps and canes, the theater is empty.

"Oh my God. No. Is that Woody Allen?" Leibowitz squints gleefully up at the screen without his glasses, his chin raised, his little Van Dyke thrust belligerently forward. "Now, there's a Jewish face for you, Belski, eh? A real *yiddishe punim!*"

I look towards the screen, its sudden brightness scalding my eyes. My head pounds as I try to decipher the images before me. As far as I can make out, the film is not a comedy but a documentary of some kind, a depiction, apparently, of the comedian's tour through Europe with a jazz band and his Asian daughter-bride.

In one scene, the reed of his clarinet gives out onstage—"So very, very Freudian!" Leibowitz nudges me in the ribs—and in the next, at a factory in Paris, needing to replace it, he offers to buy an historic clarinet from the company's museum.

The French workers at the factory refuse to part with it. "Eat ease hour 'eastorie," one of them explains.

"Ah, look at him bargaining!" Leibowitz practically spits into my ear. "Look at him wheedling and needling. Ha!"

Clouds of his cologne seem to float about my head, filling my throat and nasal passages.

"See how the cultured Europeans stand around stiffly, gawking at this nervy little yid. Look at how sickened they are by his crass Jewish materialism—look, Belski!—as he attempts to muscle his Jewish money and his Jewish fame to subvert their noble history, robbing their culture of its treasures! Ah, but it's too hilarious!" he cries, as I begin to choke.

Neither of us has eaten anything since a poorish breakfast of strong cheeses and hard-boiled eggs, and Leibowitz's breath is horrid.

"Please, Leibowitz," I manage to say, my stomach churning up into my throat, my head swimming in the vapors of his perfume, but he doesn't hear me at all and instead claws in his excitement at my knee, his long nails scratching the fabric of my pants—"This must be included in my paper for tomorrow!"—the brim of his hat once again scratching my forehead.

Squirming delightedly in his chair, writhing against me, he whispers, "Everything we've discussed for the last two days—dear God!—is on that screen!"

Perhaps it's the heat (I should never have gone out without a hat) or the smells of his breath and his cologne (which, as I say, are horrid) or his hissing, which is incessant; perhaps the events of the day have affected me more than I realized; but as I turn from the screen to confront him, to beg him, please, to desist, his glasses are now on and I see, for an intense instant, my own face reflected twice, once in each of his light-spangled lenses, and also the larger reflections of Woody Allen's luminous face superimposed upon each of mine, with Leibowitz's face behind them as a sort of frame.

As I stare, Narcissus-like, into this hydra-headed vision of Jewish faces, something erupts inside me, propelling me forward. I begin heaving the remains of my breakfast out onto the floor, splattering my shoes with a repulsive egestive keck.

"Oh! oh dear! oh God! oh, oh my goodness!" Leibowitz pounds my back, his head bent down, near my knees, to inquire, like a smarmy innkeeper, after my well-being. "Are you all right, Belski? Is there anything you need? You're not choking, are you? Are you choking? Is there anything you need?"

I try to answer, to ask him to please stop hitting my back, but his cologne and his stale breath and his scratchy beard conspire to overwhelm my senses and I cannot stop vomiting.

return to glue-eaters' island

I open the refrigerator door and Franny's lunch bag is leaning against a milk carton, its top creased and folded down with her full name, FRANCESCA GREER-BELSKI, stenciled across it in Isabelle's colorful hand. There's nothing more melancholy, I've found, than a carefully prepared object left behind, and the piercing heartbreak I experience at the sight of it overwhelms me. This is not an unfamiliar feeling. Many mornings, in fact, I've woken late to an already empty house to discover Isabelle's tea sitting in its stainless steel traveling mug, stone cold on the kitchen counter.

What hope is there in this often bitter world, I'm generally moved on these occasions to reflect, if even the little kindnesses we prepare ourselves are ineffectual?

And today, it's even worse.

Today, the late morning sun presses its cold light against the window pane, a frigid breeze stirs the curtains. Perhaps because each letter of Franny's name has been so very carefully outlined in one color and so very playfully filled in with another, the despair the bag occasions in me is more profound than usual, although I'm not entirely surprised to find it here.

Franny can be quite cranky and disagreeable in the mornings. She can be quite cranky and disagreeable all day, in fact, but it's worse in the mornings, when Isabelle, struggling against her own fatigue, is also cranky and disagreeable, her attention erratic at best, divided as it is between gathering her own things and attempting to feed and dress our somnambulistic little child before marshaling her out the door.

Having been up until nearly four myself, wrestling with an obscure passage in Mahler's *Des Knaben Wunderhorn,* the last thing I want is to make the trip out to Glue-Eaters' Island, and yet the thought of Franny, hungry and quite possibly frantic, unable to join in the Islander's sticky potlatch, is finally more than I can bear.

I throw the bag onto the passenger seat of my car and trace the route to her day care. It's midmorning already, and the entire day seems vexed. I watch a couple in a minivan behind me in my rearview mirror, when we are both stopped at the light.

The man is heavyset, with a buzz cut, and the woman sits beside him in a pink tube top and the sort of overlarge rectangular eyeglasses women used to wear in the early eighties, often with their name embossed across one of the lenses in small, glittering letters. Both of them staring, neither of them speak until at last the man reaches for something, a potato chip (I see as his hand reappears above the dash), which he places between his teeth, so that it now extends from his mouth like a salty tongue.

And it is in this posture that he turns to face the woman. It takes a moment, of course, for her to feel the burn of his gaze on her cheek, but when she does, she turns, taking his large, square head in her hands, and pulling it towards her, as though for a kiss, she eats the potato chip right from his mouth.

My own mouth falls open and I stare at them in disbelief until the light changes and they have the gall to honk at me.

At the same time, I'm listening to a radio interview with Al Green who tells the interviewer that he gave up soul for gospel music after a strange conversion experience at an Anaheim hotel. Along with his band, his entourage included not only his girlfriend, but also his father, he says, and that night, during which he and his girlfriend had decided uncharacteristically to sleep in separate suites, he was seized by an inexplicable and uncontrollable trembling. Running into the hallway, his hands and feet shaking, he pounded on his father's door.

"Daddy, look at my hands!" Al Green shouted. "Daddy, look at my feet and my hands! Daddy, look at my hands!"

And his father, folding him into his arms and grappling him to his chest, turned aside for a moment to offer up his praises. "Thank you, Lord! Thank you, Jesus, for saving my son."

"And this disturbed you?" Dr. Chaikyn asks me when I report these events to him during my analytic hour later in the day.

"It troubled me, yes," I say. "Why wouldn't it trouble me?"

He brings his small hands flat together, positioning them beneath his nose, his index fingers pressing against his lips, and a large brass ring protruding, like a swollen knuckle, from the third finger of his left hand. A halo of greyish curls encircles his high forehead like a bag of moldy cotton candy.

"Those hands and feet," I say. "I mean, what about them made Al Green's father assume that Al Green was having, not a drug overdose or a nervous breakdown, but a religious experience? Would that have been your first assumption, Dr. Chaikyn? It certainly wouldn't have been mine. And what about these other people, the man and woman in the car? I mean, how long have they been doing this thing with the potato chip? And more importantly: why? *Why* would they do it? I mean, it wasn't a spontaneous thing. I could see that by the way the woman looked at the man, without surprise or questioning of any kind. No, it was obviously something they'd done before."

"And this troubles you?"

"Yes, it troubles me!"

"Hmn," he says.

"Hmn?" I say.

"Yes," he says.

"What do you mean: hmn?" I say.

"Nothing," he says.

"Nothing?" I say.

"No," he says.

"No?" I say. "What do you mean: nothing?"

"Nothing," he says. "It's just . . . I don't understand why, having witnessed these seemingly unrelated events, you should suddenly find yourself lying on your daughter's rest mat at her day care, unable to rise or get up."

"That is the question, isn't it?"

"Is it?"

"Well, it would be, wouldn't it?"

"Hmn," he says.

"Hmn?"

"Hmn?"

"Yes," I say.

"What do you mean: hmn?" he says.

"Nothing," I say.

"No?" he says.

"No," I say and, unfortunately, this is not, for us, an atypical exchange. Many of our sessions in fact are unprofitably similar, with Dr. Chaikyn, a diminutive man, concerned primarily, or so, at least, it seems to me, with maintaining his own sense of authority. We sit, for example, facing each other in mismatched leather chairs, his raised intentionally—of this I'm absolutely certain—higher than mine, so that he's able to peer down at me, as though from a celestial height, constructing for himself an unfair psychological advantage.

"That he's a *psychologist,* Charles, is what gives him a psychological advantage, not his *chair,*" Isabelle says, crooking a finger inside her book to mark her place. She's sitting up in bed with her back against the pillows, wearing a pair of men's pajamas beneath a blue checkered robe, looking, except for the puckered sadness around her eyes, like an ingénue from a Billy Wilder film in which a single woman, locked out of her apartment for the night, is forced to sleep in the apartment of a male coworker, in a spare pair of his pajamas, while he tosses and turns on the sofa, on the other side of the locked bedroom door, pining for her chastely.

"*He's* the one with the confidentiality oath, not you!" she says when I refuse to discuss the session with her further.

But how can I, when Dr. Chaikyn and I spend almost every minute of each analytic hour discussing ways for me to leave her, a decision made even more difficult to implement most recently by her miscarriage and before that by her announcement to me that she was pregnant.

"Is one of these balls darker than the other?" she said a month or so ago, emerging from the bathroom, into which she'd sequestered herself, raising the plastic stick from her home pregnancy detection kit towards the bulb of our ceiling lamp. "Look at this with me for a minute, will you, Charles?"

She waved the little stick beneath my nose. It smelled tartly of urine and, like Proust with his Madeleine, I was immediately bombarded by a blizzarding whirl of conflicting emotions. On the one hand, I was elated at the idea of having another child; on the other hand, its birth greatly complicated my still quite secret divorce plans. There were couples, I knew, for whom the arrival of an unexpected child was reason enough to salvage a not yet irreparable marriage; although most of these, if, in fact, not all of them, had, it was clear, merely postponed a break that was inevitable, divorcing a few years later, even more bitterly, if that were possible, having wasted yet another year or two married to the wrong person. I reminded myself that the results of these tests were hardly definitive; the test itself, according to its own packaging, was no more than ninety-nine percent reliable; all of which meant only that if Isabelle *weren't* pregnant, I could leave her feeling not like a caitiff, more like a poltroon, an insignificant distinction, perhaps, but under the circumstances, it was the only distinction I could claim.

And yet, before I could compose myself sufficiently to hazard an opinion on the color of the little balls, Isabelle raced out onto the front porch where, in the natural light, the subtle differences in hue between the twin spheres in their plastic cage, the one pink, the other purple, was unmistakably distinct.

And that night, as though I were a character in a story by Sholem Aleichem, my great-grandfather appeared to me in a dream.

"S'felt unz goyim in der velt," he thundered at me in a ghostly voice, *"me darf nokh an anderer?"*

Black plumes of smoke rose from the parapets of a routed city. A hot wind blew, and there was an odd, slanted light to everything, as though, outside the field of perception allowed me by the dream, the sun were descending in cadmium flames.

"S'felt unz goyim in der velt, me darf nokh an anderer?"

I could hear the earth crumbling beneath my feet as I stepped towards the city, and then, as though he had been waiting on my arrival, my great-grandfather appeared from inside the ruins, walking the seared plains towards me in a long gabardine coat, belted with a sash, his white beard spilling like milk across his chest, until he stood before me.

At first I didn't recognize him.

I had no idea who he was until he reached into the rubble that lay at his feet and withdrew from it an empty gilt frame, holding it aloft, so that it circumscribed his head. Only then did I recognize him from the portrait that hangs on the wall of my Aunt Adelle's condominium in Chicago.

"Great-grandfather?" I said. "Is it really you?"

"S'felt unz goyim in der velt, me darf nokh an anderer?" he said for a third time, and I awoke, shivering and perspiring, certain it had been a portent.

"And you understood these words?" Dr. Chaikyn asked me.

"Certainly; I know enough German to decipher them," I said.

There aren't enough Gentiles in the world, you have to bring in another?

"*Und . . . so?*" Dr. Chaikyn said.

"*Und so, ja, genau,*" I said.

"An angry father shakes his rod at the son who refuses him proper heirs."

"That's putting it a little bleakly, isn't it?"

"Dr. Belski, may I ask you a personal question?"

"*Another* personal question, don't you mean?"

"Do you consider yourself a religious man?"

"Certainly not. Emphatically not!" I said.

And yet, one needn't believe in God in order to feel abandoned by Him. It's difficult, of course, to express a feeling like this to a Dr. Chaikyn, a Jew so assimilated he claims to celebrate every holiday on the calendar, no matter its religious provenance —"Oh, but you should have seen the veils my daughters made for this year's Ramadan," he told me once, his little feet dangling inches above the carpeting, "or the tribute to Vishnu the two scamps cooked up"—impossible to explain to a sophisticated man like him that, despite my affection and, yes, need and even my very real love for Isabelle, I can no longer remain married to her, living Zeppo-like among the stock players, as it were.

"He invented a wristwatch. Did you know that?" Dr. Chaikyn said.

"Who? What?" I said. "Who?"

"Zeppo," he said.

"What?" I said.

"Yes, after he retired from the act, he invented a wristwatch that also monitored irregular heartbeats. I read it on the SPAZ website after you mentioned him a few sessions ago."

"SPAZ?" I said.

"Apparently it stands for the 'International Society for the Prevention of Abuse toward Zeppo Marx.'"

"Ah," I said.

"Apparently, he still has his fans."

As I was saying: Who doesn't feel abandoned, stranded, shipwrecked into human life like Robinson Crusoe onto his island, forced to make order out of the natural chaos we encounter here, creating our little worlds ex nihilo, each of us against all evidence imagining himself the central hero of some significant drama, each the pinnacle of a long and heroic chain of triumphant copulations? But for what purpose? and to what end? Surely not that we may sit in our minivans and eat our potato chips from one another's mouths!

And yet in the West, in the wake of the Enlightenment, we've taken what is essentially a state of psychological pathology—the alienated, isolated ego—and conflated it with the archetype of the hero, so that each one of us is now expected, as though he were Ulysses or the Lone Ranger, to live heroically divorced from a defining culture, without a history or a community or a hierarchy of shared values, and to make of this solitary, muddled wandering a meaningful and exemplary life.

It's an impossible task and one at which we all must fail, and it's no wonder when we're all as rootless and nomadic as one of Wagner's Jews!

And so, every night, as Isabelle and Franny and I sat down to our dinner, I struggled to pronounce the simple speech I couldn't bring myself to even rehearse, the few honest words that, like a skeleton key, would free me from my prison. Holding Isabelle in bed, listening to the chaotic rhythms of her heart, I schemed to effect my self-exile from home, knowing that it had to be done, and yet, like Hamlet, I continued to temporize, while Isabelle lived in a state of high giddiness, flushed with renewed fecundity.

How could I destroy the fragile construction of her happiness?

How could I tell her that I was leaving our marriage and abandoning our daughter, not for a new life with another woman or because she herself had in any way displeased me, but because our marriage was forbidden by a pharisaical interpretation of an ancient verse of scripture claiming simply that Esau's Canaanite wives were a source of bitterness to his parents? (Genesis 26:35.)

She'd have been devastated. Or worse, enraged. She would never have stopped screaming. And I would have shamed myself by arguing an archaic religious point that I could neither fully articulate nor wholeheartedly defend.

All my life, Judaism seemed little more to me than a highly articulated form of ethnic paranoia, but now, having all but abandoned it, I couldn't help feeling its loss, as though I had been denied an ancient birthright, or had thoughtlessly traded it away for the thin gruel of modernity and an attractive wife.

I was ill-educated as a Jew, it's true, "raised in captivity," as the Sages of the Talmud say, and I wasn't proposing that I don a black hat and a black suit and quit my job and retreat, like a *bucher,* to yeshiva to learn a *blatt* of Gemara a day. But wasn't it the least I could do to populate my small portion of the earth with Jewish children?

For two thousand years, we resisted all manner of persecution and revilement, remaining unrepentantly ourselves in the face of pogroms and expulsions, forced conversions and blood libels, only to have traded it in for the high culture of Europe, surrendering it all in exchange for a few wonderfully deliriously marvelous strains of Mozart and Bach!

However, try explaining that to the ghost of your great-grandfather when he next appears to you in a dream. I could barely sleep, in fact, for fear of having to face him. And I'd only just dropped off near dawn when Isabelle, kneeling by our futon, shook me violently awake.

"Get up, Charles!" she whispered.

"What is it?" I said.

"I just weighed myself and I've lost two pounds!"

"Two?"

"Two or three!" she said. "What does it matter?"

(Apparently, no one loses weight while pregnant.)

"Of course, no one loses weight when they're pregnant. How could you even think that?" She pulled off her gown and stepped into her skirt. Hunched over, she looked skinny and pale, her breasts hanging, like two deflating balloons, from her chest.

"It can't be that uncommon," I said, searching for my pants in the dark. "Perhaps you haven't been eating enough."

"Perhaps she hasn't been eating enough," I said to Dr. Paull in his examination room.

He pressed a cold stethoscope into Isabelle's back, his face a hieroglyph of grim dissatisfaction. He wore an old-fashioned Beatle haircut liberally streaked with grey. Rubbing an ultrasound device across Isabelle's abdomen, he watched a small television screen confirming for himself what she already knew: the baby's heart had stopped.

He handed her tissues, two for her nose and several to wipe away the jelly.

Dissatisfied with our previous obstetrician, Isabelle had telephoned scores of doctors, subjecting each to a long personal, philosophical and medical inquiry before settling on Dr. Paull. We had both been charmed by his sweet temper. If only I could be born again, I often found myself thinking, brought into life a second time, eased into the world by his benevolent hands, how might my life have been different? Now, however, with a dead baby rotting inside her, Dr. Paull seemed less like one of the madcap Beatles and more like a landlord who must, against his own wishes, evict us.

We sat across from him in large, upholstered chairs, his desk a glass-covered island between us. His eyes glittered with sympathy behind the squares of his little rimless spectacles. Isabelle took my hand and squeezed it.

"I know you said you wanted only natural procedures and, of course, we could wait for your body to slough the fetus off," he said.

"However, I think it's best if . . ." he said.

"You're making the right decision," he said, after Isabelle and I, conferring as well as we could in his presence, agreed to the procedure.

"If you'll wait in the lobby, Mr. Belski," he said, stepping from behind his desk.

"Charles," Isabelle pleaded in a whisper that only she and I could hear.

"Would it be all right, Doctor," I said, "if I attend the procedure?"

"I'm afraid we don't permit it," he said, looking over his glasses at me.

"Charles, please," Isabelle said.

"Doctor," I said.

"Now, now, where would we be, Mr. Belski, if we all simply chose to ignore the rules?"

I found myself suddenly hating him. The last thing I wanted, of course, was to annoy him moments before he operated on my wife and yet (perhaps because I was planning to do it anyway) I couldn't simply abandon her. And to his credit, he relented after another pas de deux of polite wrangling and led us down the hallway to another examination room.

"He's staying, Marta," he said to the nurse when we entered.

Isabelle climbed upon the examination table. I sat on a revolving stool near Dr. Paull's elbow.

"You should feel this immediately," he said, removing the needle from Isabelle's arm. He inserted a long plastic tube into her vagina.

Her feet were in stirrups, her knees raised and bent. Her lavender underwear, hanging around her ankle, fell across her shoe.

A loud machine began to whir and Isabelle's gaze, locked in terror onto mine, unlocked as the Valium took hold. Drunk on it, she nevertheless continued to wince and moan in pain.

"All I'm doing is essentially vacuuming out her uterus," Dr. Paull said, his mouth hidden behind a white rectangular mask.

"No . . . no . . . please . . ." she cried sloppily as the machine churned and a glass cylinder filled with red liquid.

"Another minute or two, I should think. She's not feeling any of this. Or at least she won't remember it when it's over."

I realized I'd crossed my legs, involuntarily protecting my own groin.

Finally, he switched off the machine and removed the bloody tubing from between her legs. Lowering his mask, he pushed his goggles onto his head, threw his gloves into the garbage pail and shook my hand.

"She should come to in a minute, although there's no hurry. You're free to leave when you're ready. Have her abstain from intercourse for at least two weeks, and from tampons and other vaginal contaminants."

He and Marta left the room, wheeling the machine out with them.

I sat like a dunce on my stool, while Isabelle slept on the table.

Perhaps I should leave now, I thought. It's as good a time as any. I could sneak out before she wakes up and send her a short note from the International Headquarters of Chabad in Borough Park or from a settlement in the West Bank.

"Are they going to start soon?" she said groggily. Struggling to sit up, she raised herself onto her elbows, clacking her tongue against the dry roof of her mouth. She looked about the room, her face darkening with panic.

"It's over," I said.

"It's over?"

"They've done it already."

"Really?"

Falling back, she pressed the side of her face against the foam pillow strapped to the top of the examination table. With her eyes closed, she searched for my hand.

"Thank God you were here, Charles. That's all I can say."

And slightly drugged, she patted me proprietarily on the arm.

stacks of sticky lunch mats

As I tried to explain to Dr. Chaikyn, by the time I arrived at the
day care, the children were lying on their mats, some of them
sleeping, frozen in mid-whatever-they-were-doing; others continuing to squiggle and squirm. They resembled a mosqueful of
tiny Muslims in prayer and I made my way gingerly through
them, stepping on sections of the floor in the little alleyways that
separated each mat from its neighbors.

Franny was lying on her back in a corner of the room, staring
insomniacally at the ceiling, still at age five sucking her thumb,
her glasses folded carefully beside her, her hand grasping her ear.

My heart sank: if it's naptime, then lunchtime is over and I've come too late.

Wishing neither to disturb the slumbers of the other children nor to draw Franny's attention to myself, I stood in place and pointed helplessly at the lunch bag I'd brought, holding it up and silently mouthing "I've—brought—Franny's—lunch" to her teacher, Suneetha, who sat regally in a brightly patterned sari at a miniature table, scrubbing stacks of sticky lunch mats with a wet rag. When she acknowledged me, her smile was so enormously exaggerated that I had to wonder how much I had exaggerated my own.

On her back with her neck extended and her forehead near the floor, her gaze like a billiard ball moving from bank to bank, Franny tracked Suneetha's gaze upside down until it met mine, and despite all my precautions, my whispering and my hanging back, she discovered me, holding her lunch bag, like an incompetent famulus caught sneaking a rabbit into a magician's hat.

She squinted, turning her head upright. "Is that you, Daddy?" she said.

"Go back to sleep, Franny," I whispered, hunching my shoulders as though I were pretending to hide.

"I wasn't sleeping," she said, whispering more noisily than if she had spoken in full voice.

"Ssshh," I said gently.

"Franny," Suneetha cautioned her.

Whatever Isabelle had prepared for her lunch had begun to dampen, and a greasy stain mottled the bag's bottom. I removed my hand from beneath it, holding it by its flap, the grease from my palm further marring Franny's colorful name.

"They fed us already, Daddy," she whispered only slightly less loudly this time. "You didn't have to bring it."

And then she raised her arms, beseeching me for a hug.

"No, Francesca, your father cannot stay," Suneetha said, and the clipped, precise intonations of her accent reminded me of Gandhi's. "Franny must learn independence, Professor."

A great wave of sighing came off the mats from the sleeping children, like audible steam rising from a city grate. A few of them were awake but drowsing. They watched us as though we were a part of their dreaming, their eyes alert but motionless, their faces pressed impassively against their mats, drool dribbling from the sides of their mouths in transparent strings.

"Your father will go now, Francesca. Do you understand?" Suneetha clucked her tongue and Franny's face began to redden as she steeled herself, trying not to cry.

"Perhaps it would be all right if I lie here with her for just a few minutes, until she drops off," I said, although we all knew the likelihood of that. My presence here would do nothing but entice Franny further from her sleep. She'd never been much of a napper. Her mind, too active and filled with too many thoughts, seemed to wheel in ever-widening gyres whenever she lay her head upon a pillow.

Nevertheless, Suneetha acceded to my request, and I placed the lunch bag near Franny's head, moving her glasses to a safer reach, and making room for myself half on the mat and half on the hard wooden floor.

Franny curled up against me, a moony expression of triumph on her face. Lifting her knees into my solar plexus, she brought her nose near to mine. Her weak eyes gleaming, she patted my cheeks maternally with both hands, one free, the other with its thumb still stuck in her mouth.

"Goo-goo, goo-goo," she cooed happily, wiping her thumb on her pants and leaving a new flurry of salivarious brushstrokes amid the older drier ones.

"That's enough, Franny," I said.

I closed my eyes decisively, as though demonstrating for her the correct procedure and signaling an end to all conversation.

And with my eyes closed tightly in the already darkened room, I felt I would never be able to get up again. Paralyzed, stuck to my place on the floor, I listened to the burbling of the aquarium, to the huffing and sighing of sleeping children, and to the nervous scratchings of the rat inside his glass cage.

into the primordial womb

I never placed an ultimatum before her. On the contrary, call it what you will—the return of the repressed, the call of the fathers, a retreat into the primordial womb or even the felt presence of *dos pintele yid,* that mythical point of Jewish quintessence said to inhabit every Jewish soul—but for reasons that elude a final articulation, I found I simply could no longer remain married to a Gentile.

And if that meant that Isabelle's sister Oona was consigned to spend an endless series of not very merry Christmases alone, well, that had less to do with me, quite frankly, than with Paul of Tarsus, whose first-century break with the other Jewish followers of Jesus over the issue of missionizing to the Gentiles had been decisive and schismatic.

"Oh, Charles, please, don't bring up Paul of Tarsus now," Isabelle says.

"He's making you do this, isn't he! Isn't he!" Oona frets in our kitchen.

It doesn't help that Oona's husband, Rick, an ornery bear of a man, recently ended their marriage, essentially taking with him, when he went to live in the woods of upstate New York, a cadre of in-laws with whom Oona had grown used to spending the holidays.

"No, of course he isn't, Oona!" Isabelle crosses her arms. "Do you realize how insulting it is to me that you would even *think* that?"

Although perhaps I *did* put a little pressure on her.

No woman faced with the potential dissolution of her own marriage sits passively by. And it's true: I was no longer able to keep, even imperfectly, silent about my unhappiness. Still, I never asked her to renounce her faith. She had done so years before on her own. After an old priest denied her absolution if she didn't stop kissing her high-school boyfriend, she'd grown progressively disillusioned with (what she considered) the hypocrisy fundamental to the Catholicism her mother's family had foisted first upon her father, as a condition of *his* marriage to their mother, and then upon the children of their union.

And although one could have argued that conversion for the sake of marriage had as long and illustrious a tradition in their family as did Catholicism itself, Isabelle chose to focus instead on this priest and his clumsy attempts at theological blackmail.

"Because both he and I knew I wasn't going to stop kissing Stanny," she says to Oona, "but by telling him the truth, I was a sinner, whereas if I had lied about it, I could have been forgiven, so none of it made any sense to me."

"It's not supposed to make sense!" Oona cries. "That's the mystery of faith!"

"That's not what I'm talking about, Oona!"

"Yeah, and what about the way the Israelis treat the Palestinians then?"

"Oh, fuck," Isabelle sighs.

"And what about Christmas and Easter and *our childhood together?*" Oona whines so heartrendingly, it's all I can do, leaning against the cereal cupboard, not to relent from my stance, which most of our friends consider manipulative and tyrannical, in any case.

And it's not as though I can't see their point.

Belief in God and—even worse—in the narrowly patriarchal and ethnically self-flattering system of quite obviously humanly constructed rituals through which, according to those who most benefit from this system, a Jew is required to worship that God, is an intellectually embarrassing proposition—and not only to educated and secular people, whose free-thinking aversion to the abuses inherent in religious authority is justified, I should add, *only by all of recorded history,* but even among the rabbis and ministers and priests I know, all of whom seem uncomfortable with this quaintly pre-Freudian notion of a Benevolent Father in Heaven, who, though He may turn His stony back on the slaughter of millions of innocent children, nevertheless continues guiding the stars and planets in their courses, (sometimes) healing the sick and comforting the weary, (sometimes) releasing the captive, and (even, occasionally) secreting a winning lottery ticket in the pocket of a deserving adherent, as long as he is not a homosexual.

It's as though God were a professional liability to these men and women of the cloth, a crazy uncle who, unfortunately, because he owns controlling shares in the family business, can't be ignored or even chastised when he shows up, drunk and raving, at the annual stockholders' meeting or the yearly family picnic, but of whom, the rest of the time, it's best to avoid the subject.

And this is what they do, the rabbis at least, seeking refuge instead in endless debates over nonsensical points of law (for example: "How many bagel chips may one eat before having to recite the blessing over bread?") or in fiery sermons about political injustice (either: "The Arabs are terrorist dogs!" or "The Israelis are colonialist pigs!") or, more commonly, in a thousand and one empty platitudes meant to reassure those who have already committed themselves to a life of stifling prayer mumbled alongside other bored congregants in airless synagogues throughout the world (i.e.: "We are the chosen people"; "It's hard to be a Jew"; "The Law of the Eternal is perfect"; "Never forget the six million!").

"But wait! wait! Charles! please! wait!" Isabelle lifts her palms in gentle surrender. "If this is how *you* feel, how can you possibly expect me to want to take any of it on?"

And she has a point, of course. I *am* ambivalent. I'm a Jew, after all, a member of a tribe with a long history of measuring its preeminence and centrality to world events, at least in part, by the ferocious wish of others to exterminate us.

"Yes and you make it all sound so very appealing."

ISABELLE PEDALS ALONG beside me on the bike path between the boardwalk and the sea. Gulls screech above our heads, wheeling in the lowering skies as we steer home, with Franny on her training-wheeled bicycle, pedaling with all her might in an effort to remain in front of us, a giant helmet sitting like a tortoise shell upon her head.

What Oona failed to understand, I think, is that it was Isabelle herself, a devotional type since childhood, who continued to hunger for an authentic spiritual path she could not only call her own, but also now her daughter's.

"Because let's face it, Charles," she sighs, as we lock up our bikes in the garage behind our house, "among people we know, people like ourselves, God is a taboo word. It's the one thing no one feels comfortable speaking about to their children."

To do so (as I've explained) is to place oneself in a zany, insane or fundamentalist camp, like devotees of Krishna in their saffron robes, still, after all these years, passing out vegetarian cookbooks in the lobby at LAX, or the ultra-Orthodox in Jerusalem throwing stones at violators of the Sabbath, or David Koresh self-immolating with the Branch Davidians in Waco, or even the administrators at my own Cabesa de Vaca High School in Karkel, who, when I complained to them, claimed that the morning devotionals recited over our PA system in the name of their Lord Jesus Christ didn't violate the recent Supreme Court ban on school prayer because, "Frankly, Belski, these prayers aren't prayers, but devotionals, you see?"

"Ah," I said, happy at last to have had the distinction explained to me and to the students who complained alongside me, Babi Chanda, a Buddhist, and Billy Maynard, a Protestant who no longer believed. It was clear to us, as we sat in the office of our high school vice principal, that religion served only to make an otherwise sensible person foolish, venal, violent, corrupt, intolerant or naïve.

And yet, as Isabelle plaintively frames the question, "What are the rest of us supposed to do, then, with our longing for God?"

And: how are we to raise our children?

"Because children need a spiritual grounding," Isabelle never tires of reminding me, aware that I will neither permit Franny to accompany her to a church, where she herself has no interest in taking her, nor to a zendo.

And this is what Oona fails to understand.

Isabelle herself began searching for a synagogue—I had nothing to do with it—and it was the women in her Animals in Your Chakras group who recommended a rabbi whose neo-Jungian interpretations of the Holy Writ appealed to her when she encountered them at the Torah circle he led every other Saturday morning at Makom Ohr HaLev, listed in our Yellow Pages as "A Synagogue for Jewish Meditation."

The congregation met twice a month in an unused church in Encino, where Rabbi Immanuel Falconer lectured literally for hours on the soul and the ego and the dissolving self. His congregants, numbering into the small hundreds, sang and danced and chanted, as a highlight of their service, the word *shalom* three times in unison, as though they were a *sangha* of Buddhists with a slight speech defect.

Isabelle demonstrated it for me one time, chanting nasally and sitting cross-legged with her head bowed, and her hands splayed, like dead birds, in her lap.

"Oh, Belski, you've got to hear this!" she said. "The word just rolls and rolls all around you and through you, it fills up the room, and Franny loves it there, she just *loves* it there, don't you, Franny?"

Sucking on her thumb, negotiating the conversational distance between her parents, and unwilling to choose between them, Franny raised a small shoulder to her ear and shrugged.

"Oh, the music is wonderful in a naïve sort of way, and they're highly accepting of non-Jews. I asked, Charles, and they said it was okay. I mean, you've got to come with us, you have to!"

(Allow me to regress for a moment here to explain, as perhaps I should have earlier, that this Animals in Your Chakras group Isabelle belongs to is exactly that: a therapy group, open to a small number of women, who, through trance or hypnotic suggestion, endeavor to discover and ultimately communicate with the numinous "animals" inhabiting their chakras, those wheel-like vortices of energy that, according to Eastern mystical tradition, exist in the surface of one's etheric double. I can't vouch for the work's precise methodology; I can only report, however, that, resident in her own heart, brow and navel chakras Isabelle found, respectively, a shell-less turtle named Rusty, a slug named Dumbor and a white dove called Ariella. For a complete report on the therapeutic benefits of these encounters, I refer you to Isabelle herself.)

What I can say here is that despite her daughter's indifference and her husband's reluctance to accompany her there and her sister's refusal to hear anything about it, Isabelle could no longer deny the sense of belonging she'd begun to feel at Makom Ohr HaLev.

"*Not* that I'm thinking about converting, Charles, because I'm *not*," she hastened to add. "And I want to be clear about that. I'm a monotheist and a universalist and I don't mind raising Franny as a Jew, if that will make you happy, but *I* am not a Jew, I'm not Jewish, I never will be and that's just something you're going to have to learn to live with, okay?"

AND YET, AT the same time, Isabelle began experiencing a series of strange events that she couldn't help but interpret as nudges given her in that general direction by a Celestial Hand.

The first time she heard Rabbi Falconer intoning Kiddush at the *oneg* following Friday night services, for instance, the blessing had sounded oddly familiar to her. She couldn't place it. Still, she couldn't help feeling that she had heard it her entire life.

"I knew I *knew* it, Charles," she says, as we lie in bed, ignoring the books we hold: she, Ken Wilber's *A Brief History of Everything;* and I, *The Complete Idiot's Guide to Learning Yiddish.* "It was weird and I didn't want to say anything at the time, but now I feel I can talk about it."

Leaning on her arm and propping her head up with her hand, she tells me that the experience reminded her of a night thirty years ago when, staying up late with Oona against their Grammy's wishes to watch *The Late, Late, Late Show,* they had chanced upon a film whose title and plot Isabelle can't recall, but which contained a scene she's never been able to forget: a group of Hasidic men seated around a table, pounding on its surfaces while chanting long and complicated melodies.

She presses her book against her chest, and from its covers, Ken Wilber's bald and bespectacled head stares out at me.

"I couldn't have been more than eight or nine, but I was mesmerized and stirred, profoundly so, by this wild music. It was so free and primitive, almost aboriginal, in fact, and I remember thinking, 'What *is* this?' you know? I mean, 'What *is* this?' because I'd never heard anything like it before in my life."

(Expecting to hear it again, indeed, ecstatic over the possibility of hearing it again, the first time I'd taken her to our decidedly non-Hasidic shul in Karkel, during a brief and tense visit with my parents, she'd been dismayed when a freshly scrubbed quartet of music students from the Karkel College of Agricultural Technology, led by our cantor, Mr. Blum, appeared in black formal robes to sing what were essentially church madrigals in their highly trained voices.

"This is not Jewish music!" Isabelle cried indignantly, as though she were a scholar who'd been studying its ethnology for years and whose small research stipend I'd squandered by bringing her here.

"It most certainly is!" I hissed back in my own defense. "I should know, shouldn't I? I've been listening to it my entire life!")

"And that's not the only time something like that happened," Isabelle says.

Once, she tells me, when she was a kid, a girl named Kathleen O'Grady chased her around the Our Lady of Imminent Victory Elementary School playground, shouting, "You're Jewish! Admit it, Isabelle. You're Jewish! You're not fooling anyone!"

"Don't you think that's a little weird, Charles?" She places her book on the nightstand and turns off her light. "And even then—I mean, even then, although I knew she was trying to offend me, I couldn't understand why I was supposed to be offended. I couldn't understand why being Jewish was supposed to be bad."

On the contrary, as a girl growing up in Riverdale, Isabelle envied the elements of Jewish culture that surrounded her.

"I used to walk into Strietkof's Bakery around the corner from where we lived and—oh, my God, Charles!—I'd just stare at those gorgeous loaves of rye bread, my mouth watering, wondering why were we eating Wonder bread and all these bland foods when, around the corner, this food was available, and not only available, but for sale."

(Her mother's idea of a salad was a piece of iceberg lettuce with a blob of mayonnaise on it.)

"When I had my first macaroon," she recalls, as though she were Aldous Huxley recalling his first tab of LSD, "all I could think was, 'Why has nobody told me about this before?' I've always loved halvah and herring and gefilte fish," she says, counting on her fingers, and pronouncing *gefilte* with a soft *g*, despite my constantly correcting her.

"Okay, and then on top of all that," she says, "why did Baruch hand me that flyer on the beach that day, even when I told him I wasn't Jewish?"

(A short, giggling man with kinky red hair under a burgundy yarmulke, Baruch had skimmed through a large crowd of buskers and passersby on the boardwalk at Venice Beach to ask Isabelle if she were by any chance Jewish, ignoring the rest of us who stood around her waiting for a table at the Plum Tree.

"Really?" he giggled, after having introduced himself. "Are you certain? Well, here. Take this anyway." And, as though it were a bouquet of roses, he handed her a green flyer announcing a series of lectures that promised to reveal the origins of the universe and the mysteries of the soul in a small number of inexpensive weekly classes.)

"Well, that's easy enough to explain." I pull the bedsheets to my chin. Men are always making exceptions for Isabelle, often quite drastic ones, and apparently even cherubic Baruch with his velveteen yarmulke and his ringling earlocks and his fifteen hours of kabbalistic permutations a day hadn't risen sufficiently above the material plane to remain insensitive to Isabelle's physical charms.

"Oh, that's just bullshit, Charles, that's just bullshit, and you know it." Sitting up in bed, Isabelle throws off the covers and waves her arms in front of her as though to dispel an unpleasant odor. "And it's just so demeaning!"

And yet, I remain convinced that it was for this reason and this reason alone that we found ourselves, not long afterwards, in a cramped storefront on Robertson, two of six or seven people, listening to a pale, bearded man in a creased suit explain the basics of Lurianic Kabbalah, delving (with a precise sense of unintelligible detail) into the husks of impurity, the sparks of holiness and the primordial vessels which, unable to contain God's Infinite Light, shattered at the instant of Creation.

"Each and every Jewish soul," Rabbi Rakia Pa'amoni said in his incomprehensible Israeli accent, "must work to free these hidden sparks of light, liberationing them— is the word, yes?— liberationing them?—and ourselves from the impure husks, the *klippot*—the shells?—restoring wholeness to the upper and to lower spheres."

"Now, you say 'Jewish soul'"—Isabelle raised her hand— "but what is the role of the non-Jewish soul in all of this?"

"That is many complicated questions," Rabbi Pa'amoni said. Sucking on his mouche, he looked with slitted eyes towards Baruch, who, reddening even more than usual, blushed beneath his burgundy yarmulke and giggled in his seat.

"Why didn't you tell me all this was in Judaism, Charles?" Isabelle asked as we drove through the streets of West LA, more excited than I'd seen her in years.

"I had no idea," I said. And this was true. Somehow, during the many Friday nights I spent as a child in our little shul in Karkel, between Rabbi Kleinblatt's periodic tirades against Arabs and his even less infrequent outbursts against our cantor, Mr. Blum, the mystical structures of the universe never came up.

dozens of attempted reschedulings

As it happened, Rabbi Pa'amoni was only the first of Isabelle's many rabbis. Rabbi Falconer was the second.

Dissatisfied as a young man with pulpit work, he had returned to school for a doctorate in psychology and now owned a chicken farm in Topanga Canyon, where, on any given day, he spent a third of his time studying Native American spiritual practices, a third tending to his clients' psyches, and a third candling eggs.

Working only on the side as a rabbi, he studied with Isabelle two or three mornings a week, grilling her in Hebrew syntax and grammar while she hauled feed and lent a hand with various other farm chores.

Over lunch, they analyzed the weekly Torah portion, interpreting its revolving constellations of characters as though they were figures in an ancient god's dream: Moses' murder of the Egyptian is the psychic killing each of us must do of his false or assimilated self; Pharaoh is the shadow side of Moses' own lust for power; Hagar and Ishmael represent the negative aspects of ourselves that we split off and deny.

"Everything Freud and Jung discovered about the psyche"— Rabbi Falconer tapped his earth-blackened fingernail against the pristine margin of the text—"the writers of the Torah knew. My God, Isabelle, it's all here."

Even I will admit there was a vitality at Makom Ohr HaLev unlike anything I'd experienced in a synagogue. The music was in fact stirring, and Rabbi Falconer's heroically long sermons did in fact seem to effect a deep psychological shift in his congregants. In their colorful prayer shawls and yarmulkes, men and women swayed to the music, their arms draped around one another's shoulders, many of them in tears by evening's end.

And yet, the entire enterprise stuck me as comic and absurd.

Is it quibbling to say that the sight of Isabelle, a lapsed Catholic, chanting a Hebrew word like a Buddhist in a quorum of Jews before a cross hanging in the chancel of a church built on land stolen from Indians didn't strike me as an authentically Hebraic act of worship? Certainly, if my great-grandfather had dared to show his face there, he would only have been disoriented. (I cringe at the thought of having to explain *this* to him in a dream.) And yet, Isabelle had never seemed happier. In fact, she seemed to be getting more out of the religion than I had thought possible. I should have been pleased, I suppose, but instead, I found myself repelled by the enthusiasm with which she embraced Judaism, an enthusiasm that seemed to me distinctly un-Jewish.

Growing tan and muscular in her shorts and T-shirts, she'd become something of a fixture on the Falconer farm, a devoted pupil to the rabbi, a sister to his wife, and an honorary aunt to their brood of small children.

"*Oi, gey veys!*" she shouted happily, accenting the phrase oddly. "It's like working on a kibbutz, Charles. *Gotteynu!* I feel like one of the *halutzim!*"

She loved these days, in fact, and would have studied with Rabbi Falconer indefinitely, had her extensive reading into the history of Judaism not left her jaundiced about the authenticity of its enlightenment reforms, and when she revealed to Rabbi Falconer that she was thinking about converting, she couldn't help confessing her doubts to him as well.

"I hate to say this, Manny, but with the assimilationist history of the Reform movement, don't you think an Orthodox or at the very least a Conservative conversion is pretty much de rigueur, especially if I'm thinking about moving to Israel?"

"Are you?"

"Well, no, but, I mean, you have to leave your options open. And it *is* a mitzvah to inhabit the land."

Half-hoping he would argue her out of her concerns, she was surprised by his reaction. Putting down his axe, he kicked at his woodpile, sighed, and, looking towards the sea, recommended she talk to a colleague of his, an Orthodox rabbi named Emmanuel Gurwitz.

"It's political, of course," he said, "but what about Jewish life isn't?"

ALTHOUGH, LIKE A good Hasid, Isabelle was more than happy to follow her rebbe's instructions, Rabbi Gurwitz proved difficult to approach. When Isabelle finally got through to him on the phone, he refused to even meet with her and he also called Rabbi Falconer a loon.

"Did he tell you all that crap about Freud and the so-called writers of the Torah?" he asked during this initial conversation. "Because listen, dearie, let me tell you something about Freud: Freud was nothing but a self-hating Jew, exactly like that husband of yours, because why else would he have married someone like you, right?"

"He doesn't seem spiritual at all," Isabelle confided to me. "I mean, how can he be an Orthodox Jew and not be spiritual?"

But because Rabbi Falconer, whom she greatly respected, insisted it was all for show—"He's only doing this to discourage you, Isabelle, as traditional Jewish law requires with a potential convert."—Isabelle persisted and finally Rabbi Gurwitz agreed to speak with her in person.

However, he broke their appointment without warning, as he did dozens of attempted reschedulings, so that it was quite a while before they actually met, and when they did, he greeted her brusquely without looking at her or rising from behind his desk.

"Sit down, sit down, sit down." He picked a black hair from his black beard off the black lapel of his black suit and scowled at her blackly. "Remind me what it is that you want with me again, Miss——?"

"Belski."

"Belski?" He sniffed suspiciously.

Exhaling to calm herself, Isabelle screwed up her nerve and reiterated for him the series of events that had led her to seek him out: her marriage to me, my midlife regrets, the scene in *The Late, Late, Late Show,* being chased around the schoolyard by Kathleen O'Grady, Baruch and her classes with Rabbi Pa'amoni, her sensation upon eating her first macaroon. And though Rabbi Gurwitz snorted dismissively through most of it — disparaging what she had learned with Rabbi Falconer as *narishkeit* and impugning Rabbi Pa'amoni and the Scientific Centre for Kabbalistic Research as "a den of antireligious charlatans offering a cut-rate Judaism to unsuspecting and ignorant Jews" (like me) and, even worse, "to goyim, such as yourself, no offense, who have no business blackening our sacred texts with their dirty paws"—in the end, he offered to work with her "provisionally," making no promises of the results, "if, at this point, that's still something you would like to do."

"However," he added, "I can tell you frankly that out of every five hundred people who approach me with this stupid notion of becoming Jewish, only one finishes the process, and from the looks of it, I don't imagine that one will be you."

"Can you believe the arrogance and the presumptuousness of that horrible man?" Isabelle railed against him for hours, and I imagined this would be the end of it, but, to my dismay, Isabelle seemed strangely invigorated by the challenges Rabbi Gurwitz laid before her. She seemed to blossom under his strict exercitations, resisting them less and less as time went on.

As far as I was concerned, the man was a doxological nightmare.

Along with the (relatively) harmless laws of kashrut and the weave of the sacred calendar and the order of the prayer book, Isabelle began receiving under his fiery tutelage, an unhealthy dose of right-wing fundamentalism masquerading as scientific rationalism.

Through supposedly irrefutable and logical proofs, he convinced her that God's existence was a demonstrable fact, and that His authorship of the Torah (with Moses working, Watson-like, as his amanuensis) was a matter of empirical proof as well.

"Think of it, Isabelle"—he tapped his soft, sun-deprived finger against the pristine margin of the text—"if the Torah were merely stories written by human beings, don't you think we could have done a better job?"

"Yeah, Charles," Isabelle parroted him later that evening during one of our interminable arguments on the subject, "if the Torah were written by men, do you really think the Jews who wrote it would have depicted themselves in such an unflattering light?"

But this is something, I hastened to remind her, that we Jews have been doing consistently in our writing ever since.

"When a Jew reads the Torah," she said, "it's like a cake reading its own recipe."

And what exactly does a cake do with this sort of information? I wondered.

"*Gevalt*," she said, "if the goyim only knew how much depended on Jews keeping the mitzvahs, they'd follow us around —well, they'd follow you around; I'm not Jewish yet—begging you to perform them."

What had I done? I had to wonder.

This was not the Isabelle I knew and loved.

A part of me had hoped this encounter with Rabbi Gurwitz might send her scrambling back to the bland and inoffensive gnosticism she had for so long embraced.

"Back to Makom and Rabbi Falconer, Charles, which you hated and laughed at and mocked?"

I was willing to drop my insistence that she convert, if only we could have our former lives returned to us.

And yet nothing I said or did seemed to make the slightest impression on her, and I could only stand by, horrified, as I watched her surrender her powers of discrimination and autonomy to Rabbi Gurwitz who, as part of her indoctrination into his medievalist worldview, insisted she take upon herself a rigid standard of ritual observance, as a consequence of which she covered her hair and began wearing full skirts and long sleeves, forcing me to sleep apart from her whenever she was menstruating.

"The way women allow themselves to be treated in this society is a scandal, Charles. I mean, the West has literally brainwashed women into thinking they're free — no, it has — feeding them all this bullshit about equality and liberation, while inviting them onto tabletops to dance nude in bars."

She forbade me to turn a light on or off or even to listen to music on Saturdays, so that every Saturday, I sat alone in our dark house, waiting for her to return with Franny from the Orthodox synagogue to which they walked each week.

I could have driven somewhere or gone out, of course, but the look of reproach she gave me the first two times I tried it made me feel too guilty to attempt it for a third.

Not only was I setting a poor example for our daughter, but worse, I was now, in Isabelle's eyes, at least, one of those benighted secular Jews who, in refusing to heed the commandments of his Creator, prevented not only the coming of the Messiah but the consequent redemption of the entire fallen world.

It was much simpler to sit in the dark, and this is what I did each week, wondering each week, in despair, what had happened to the spirit of inquiry and intellectual skepticism I'd always associated with Judaism. Where was the love of free thought I'd been taught was essential to the religion of Einstein and Maimonides?

"My God, these people don't even accept the theory of evolution, Isabelle!" I raged one Friday evening as Isabelle attempted to light the Shabbos candles according to Rabbi Gurwitz's precise instructions. "Explain to me, if you will, exactly what bad wigs and beards have to do with redeeming the universe through states of heightened spiritual awareness?"

Intentionally I threw her former concerns into her face.

And it was true, from the outside, at least, the piety of Rabbi Gurwitz's community seemed little more than a matter of sartorial affectation, the men barbaled in dark suits and Borsalinos, the women intentional dowds in amorphous skirts, turbans and snoods.

"They dress that way out of modesty, Charles."

"By modestly calling attention to themselves for their own extraordinary piety?"

"You choose to see it that way."

"I choose to see it."

"And you don't wear a uniform, I suppose?"

"An invisible uniform, yes, and therefore a modest uniform. Can't you see, Isabelle, it's nothing more than a nostalgic game of dress-up, a sentimental post-Holocaust masquerade with everyone showing up as a fantasy version of his own grand-father!"

"*Sha,* Charles! You're giving me a headache!" Glaring at me, she bundled two loaves of challah beneath a velvet cloth and set them in the center of the table. Franny climbed into her lap, her hair in fresh-washed curls, her glasses gleaming against the light of the Shabbos candles.

I had to admit they looked radiant together.

Resting her chin on the crown of Franny's head, Isabelle said, "Well, are you going to make Kiddush for us or not, Mr. Belski?"

"I have no problem with that," I said. I took the prayer book-let from her hand, and found the correct page. Standing, I poured the wine and lifted the glass and recited the lengthy blessing, struggling with the Hebrew at first but remembering it after all.

The tune my grandfather used to sing for it came back to me easily. Standing at the head of his own dining room table, a silver goblet in his manicured hand, he recited Kiddush every Friday night in Karkel for my grandmother, my father, my mother, my sisters and me. A large man, always in a suit and a tie with a diamond stickpin, his thinning hair dyed immaculately black each week by a barber at the In-Towne Inn, he wore glasses, I realized, exactly like Franny's, and as I sang, I could almost feel him standing at my side. I heard his voice in my ear. And beside him, I felt the presence of *his* father, a lumber merchant from Poland, bearded in a long caftan, the father of ten, murdered—

with his wife and five of their children, their children's spouses and their children's children—by the Nazis. His voice was low and melodious and, beside him, I could feel *his* father. I saw our faces as though they were different versions of the same face, stretched and modeled and padded according to epoch and custom. The nose pulled out here or turned there, the mouth full or thin, the chin bearded or clean-shaven, the eyes similar in every generation.

It's difficult to speak of these things, of course, but somehow I felt as though I were standing in my own family's version of Leibowitz's Model of Assimilating Man, no longer like Zeppo, my chest thrust forward in the vanguard; now more like Groucho, the tails of my cutaway rising on either side of me as I fall back inside the ghetto walls.

And then, of course, the impression faded, and though I had experienced it myself, I could barely credit its having happened.

the ultimatum

"So, when are we going to meet this husband of yours, this Charles Belski we've all heard so much about?" Rabbi Gurwitz finally asks Isabelle, as I knew he finally would.

"Just don't do anything to embarrass me, okay?" Isabelle says, on the drive to his house, leaning in from the passenger seat to adjust her hat in the rearview mirror. "Sorry to have to be so blunt."

"What are you talking about?" I say. "When have I ever embarrassed you?"

"You're joking, right? Daddy's joking, isn't he, Mommy?" Franny says from her car seat in back.

"I don't think so, Franny."

"You do it all the time, Daddy."

"Not all the time, Franny."

"Well, but pretty often, right, Mommy?"

"Pretty often," Isabelle says. "But, I mean, not too often. But let's not make him feel any more uncomfortable than he already is, okay, because that'll only make it worse."

THE HOUSE IS OLD and small, on a corner lot in the Pico-Robertson district.

Rabbi Gurwitz answers the door and ushers us in. "Welcome, welcome," he says, and I'm surprised to see how young he is, barely past thirty. For some reason, I had expected an older man with a long white beard.

"Yeah, I get that all the time," he says.

Isabelle blushes.

"Anyway, anyway, come in, come in, come in."

He leads us into the dining room, where a long table has been set with a white cloth covered in plastic sheeting. An assembly of mismatched chairs surrounds it. Vertical plastic blinds cover the windows from ceiling to floor, and on every side of the room, bookshelves groan under heavy, gilt-edged volumes.

Rabbi Gurwitz removes his large black hat; beneath it, he wears another hat, a small velvet yarmulke. A deep red indentation shows in his forehead where the hat has bitten into it.

"Allow me to introduce you to my wife," he says, gesturing to a squat woman with a lolling bosom in a dowd's dress and an amorphous turban on her head, whose heavy eyeglasses keep falling to the bottom of her nose.

"So happy to meet you finally, Professor."

She ignores the hand I offer her, staring away from it, as though it held a fish.

"Charles," Isabelle says, folding my palm inside hers.

"Right, of course," I say.

"Men and women don't touch, Daddy."

"Sorry," I say, and against my will, a hostile tone creeps into my voice. Franny raises her eyebrows in a silent reprimand.

"If they were Amish or Ibo," Isabelle scolds me in a whisper, "you'd be curious and charmed."

"But they're not, are they?" I whisper back.

Rabbi Gurwitz seats us at the end of the table, and the rest of the chairs immediately fill with his children, eight or nine or ten of them. I never get an accurate count.

"Yemini in Mookie are learning it near Israel," he says, or something along those lines, nodding towards the bank of his remaining sons. They sit like mimeographed copies of one another, all in white shirts and black vests, their little skullcaps on their round heads, the older few wearing identical pairs of eyeglasses, all of them with ritual fringes snaking out from their shirt waists in a visual counterpoint to the coiled earlocks that sprout from their temples.

The rebbetzin and her daughters, colorful blurs of femininity, rush in and out of the kitchen, carrying bowls and platters on their arms. Franny and Isabelle rise to lend a hand, and the men are left to sit and discuss the Torah.

It's a pleasant enough evening, although, in all honesty, by the end of it, my neck aches from keeping balanced the little yarmulke they've given me. Light and flimsy, it continually drifts off my head, and I struggle again and again — stupidly, in fact — to catch it before it hits the ground.

"Oh, but this is idiotic!" I say, snatching the scrap of fabric from the carpeting. "How are you supposed to wear these idiotic things?"

"Daddy," Franny whispers. "Remember . . . what we said . . . in the car?"

Finally, I ball the slip of fabric up in my fist and slap it against my scalp, where I feel it springing up on the ends of my hair.

"I KNOW, I KNOW," Isabelle whispers as we lie in bed. The Gurwitzes have given us a room to ourselves (Franny is sleeping down the hall with the children) and the rebbetzin has covered the night-light with a dishcloth, so that we have a little light, but not too much to sleep.

"They're fanatics. Of course, they're fanatics. Even I can see that, Charles, but you know what?" She turns and strokes my arm. "At least they're happy."

The night-light gleams off the white sheets, outlining the cellolike curves of her body.

"I'm glad to hear you say this," I say.

"I admit I may have gotten a little carried away." Lying on her back, she stares at the halo of light splashed across the ceiling. "Rabbi Gurwitz and his family, the people in this community—no, you're right, Charles—they live in a mythological world. They do. They live *inside* their mythology in a way that you and I simply can't and never will. They're like Aboriginal bushmen, wandering around in Dream Time, believing all these remarkable things."

"I know. It's crazy," I say.

"But when you think of it," Isabelle says, "I mean, what's the point of believing that life is meaningless and random, if it's only going to make you feel miserable?"

"Well," I say.

"I don't know about you, Charles, but I can't live like that anymore." She raises up on one elbow and looks me in the eye. "Things have got to definitely change if I'm going to feel comfortable remaining in this marriage."

"Are you giving me an ultimatum?" I say.

"No, I wouldn't call it that," she says.

"No, and why not?" I say.

"Because you'd probably find the term offensive."

THERE ARE SERVICES in the morning, followed by another meal and further religious conversations, followed by a class and another service, and a meal and another service, and then, finally, at the end of what seems like the entire five thousand years of Jewish history, Rabbi Gurwitz makes Havdalah, turns on his cell phone and bids us *gut vokh*.

"Come to my offices on Monday," he says at the door, concealing a grin inside the bristling black garden hedge of his beard, "and we'll talk about the actual conversions."

"Really?" Isabelle is suddenly nervous and pleased.

"It's time, my dear, don't you think?"

At his office, seated at his desk beneath a picture of the Temple Mount, he goes over the essential things, formalities for the most part, telling us, for instance, that because our previous marriage will now be null and void, we will have to be married again.

"Okay, all right," I say, surprised but not unnerved.

Isabelle takes my hand and squirms happily in her chair.

The ceremony needn't be elaborate, Rabbi Gurwitz continues, it requires only the presence of two witnesses—"Two witnesses, all right," I say, nodding—and he'd be pleased to conduct it himself or to recommend someone else, if that's what we wish—"God, please, yes: somebody else!" I'm thinking when I hear him say—but only after we have lived apart for three months.

"Excuse me?" I say.

"But only after you have lived apart for three months," he says again.

"Live apart for *three months?*" I look in astonishment at him and at Isabelle. "What in God's name are you talking about?"

"Charles," Isabelle cautions me.

"Okay, okay, I'll take the lenient view," Rabbi Gurwitz says.

"Excellent, the lenient view," I say. "And what exactly is the lenient view?"

"Charles," Isabelle says again.

"You may remain together in the same house, but you must never be in the same room alone, you may not talk alone together, and you must give me a key, knowing that I can drop in on you at any moment. Also, I'm forbidding you to sleep in the same room or to even touch each other under any circumstances. And Franny," he says to Franny, whom we have dragged along, unable to find a sitter, "I'm empowering you, my little friend, to watch over them and make sure they follow my instructions to the letter. Do you hear me? To the letter."

Franny pushes her bulky glasses higher onto her nose and salutes him like a little lieutenant.

And over the course of the next three months, beneath her eagle-eyed gaze, deprived of all intimacy with my wife, exiled from our familiar patterns of behavior, from our ability to even console or amuse each other, I watch as our marriage crumbles into dust, like an ancient ruin.

And then, preparatory to the ceremony, Isabelle submerges herself, as all converts must, in the waters of the *mikveh* with Franny, who, despite Rabbi Gurwitz's precise instructions to submerge three times, submerges herself four times, because, as she tells me later, she wanted to be more Jewish than her mother.

"When I met you, I had no doubt you'd comply with all this," Rabbi Gurwitz confesses to me, taking me aside before the wedding.

"And why is that?" I say.

"Because love cuts short a lot of arguments, doesn't it, my friend?"

por qué llorax la blanca niña

According to Leibowitz, who flew in from Sebastopol with his wife for the occasion, Yiddish comedies often end with a wedding. Weddings, in fact, so captivated the Yiddish imagination that many Yiddish tragedies, although they did not, perhaps, conclude with a wedding, contained scenes of weddings as well.

"*The Dybbuk*, of course, is the most famous example," he says, buttonholing me at the reception. "The play is replete with weddings and near-weddings!"

And these stagings, he tells me, became something of a headache for the local rabbinate at the time.

"Well, perhaps not in the larger cities like Kraków and Warsaw, where we ourselves were, Belski." His eyes moisten at the memory of our time together. "But a headache certainly in the smaller towns, in the shtetlach where these troupes toured and performed for our undereducated and naïve ancestors."

Simply stated, the problem was this: for a man to marry a woman in accordance with Jewish law he must give her an item of some small value, a ring, for example, and recite in Aramaic, 'Behold! I consecrate you to me in accordance with the laws of Moses and Israel.' If he does this before two qualified witnesses, then he and the woman are married.

"Now!" Leibowitz smacks his tongue after a quick tumbler of whiskey, popping a salmon canapé into his mouth and leaving an explosion of pastry crumbs in a ring around his mustache and beard. "When an actor playing a role gives a ring, though it be a mere stage prop, to an actress in character beneath a wedding canopy, though it is only part of a set, reciting this formula verbatim, for the sake of realism, before an audience of Jews, among whom, in all likelihood, sit at least two qualified witnesses, then, as far as our rabbis were concerned, the performers were legally married."

And with issues of bigamy and adultery at stake, the rabbis insisted upon divorcing the actors immediately following each performance, refusing to permit the tour to move on otherwise.

"Of course"—Leibowitz coughs and clears his throat; the

comb-over he has cultivated since I last saw him loosens and falls about one shoulder in a scraggly hank—"this naturally brings up questions of identity and intention."

He is wearing a voluminous heliotrope tuxedo with tails, a puce cummerbund and iridescent mother-of-pearl cuff links the size of Kennedy half-dollars. His voice grows stentorian as we both scan the crowd, he for others before whom he could blather and I for someone who might rescue me from his pontifications.

Everyone—my sisters, my father and his Montanan wife, her farm-fed children, various of our friends and colleagues—seems to be paying exclusive attention to Isabelle. Still carrying her bouquet and greeting our guests, even she fails to meet my eye.

"Pay attention here, Belski!" Leibowitz declaims, when it becomes clear he'll find no other audience. "The question persists: If I, as an actor, recite words I do not personally mean while pretending to be someone else, can these words actually or legally bind me? Now you would say 'Of course not!' And yet, consider. Not only do many actors speak of the importance of committing all their psychological and emotional resources to the lives they portray onstage—Stanislavski's famous Method is predicated on this single and singular premise—but many people live their *actual* life without emotional or intentional commitment to it of any kind! I needn't name names here, but you and I certainly know a few of these, don't we? eh? yes? emmm? Given this, the rabbinic stance, while seeming at first doltishly pragmatic, is not as far-fetched as you had at first assumed, and if nothing else, our sages knew the power of a ritual, eh?"

Apparently sensing my distress, Rabbi Gurwitz crosses the room and, grabbing Leibowitz by the hand, leads him into a circle of dancing men.

"'When my cue comes, call me and I will answer!'" he shouts over his shoulder. "'Every man look o'er his part, for . . . um, something, something . . . our play is preferred!'"

I down a whiskey, and moving through the buzzing crowd of well-wishers, I have to admit that his words rankle.

He's right, of course. Who am I kidding? How is it possible that Isabelle could have changed her identity and is now somehow a Jew? Have we done anything more than perform in a silly comedy that has duped a group of credulous rabbis? (For I feel certain that this is what Leibowitz is implying.) Everyone knows that Jewish law frowns on conversions for the sake of marriage. A marital convert isn't considered wholehearted. And rightly so, for who can change his essential nature? Even Mahler admitted, as he exited St. Stephen's after his conversion, that he had "changed his coat and nothing more."

And yet, it occurs to me, Jewish law itself provided Isabelle with this conversion. How could it not be authentic? It must be authentic; otherwise Rabbi Gurwitz would never have gone through with it. And if it's convincing to him, how could it not convince everyone? Even more: if the wedding between Yiddish actors on the stages of Poland were binding, how could ours not be? Perhaps I've misunderstood Leibowitz. Perhaps he meant well after all. In fact, I can only recognize these doubts as my own. Certainly they went through my head not more than an hour ago as I stood beneath the wedding canopy with Rabbis Gurwitz and Falconer, Rabbi Falconer in crisp black jeans and an embroidered Salvadoran peasant shirt, a tall Bucharan skullcap bobby-pinned above his long, grey ponytail. The fabric of his colorful woven vest shone with hundreds of tiny mirrors sewn into it. Rabbi Gurwitz was immaculate in an all-black suit, his black shoes shining until they were almost silver, his large black hat sitting atop his head as though it were a crown.

Unable to choose between them, Isabelle had asked both to perform the ceremony, and she had been surprised when each agreed.

IF YOU WERE to ask Isabelle what moved her most about the wedding, she would mention two things, the first being Rabbi Falconer's wailing. Approximately a third of the way through the ceremony, he looked at me impishly, drew in a large breath and shrieked out, as though he were a Choctaw, a piercing warrior's cry that rent the air in two.

"Aaaaaiiiiii-yiiiiii-aiiiiiiiiiiiiiiiiiiii!" he said, or words to that effect. The hair on the back of every neck stood up and bristled, I'm certain, as we each tried to synthesize the piercing sound, which, as it continued, began to change, becoming less Native American and more Eastern European in tone, quite lyrical and sad, really, and filled somehow with all the longing and beauty of the lost Ashkenazic world.

Quite slowly, the cry evolved into a blessing (I recognized the familiar pattern of Hebrew words) and even Rabbi Gurwitz seemed stirred by the primitive sound.

As his chanting attained its climax, I looked at Isabelle. Her eyes closed in a quiet ecstasy, she seemed almost to swoon, her body limp, her knees buckling, her torso sliding forward as though pushed by an unseen hand. Having felt the presence of her long-dead parents enter the wedding canopy, as she would tell me later, she was astonished to hear Rabbi Falconer say, "We welcome the souls of Isabelle's mother and father, and also of Charles's mother who join us now beneath the *chupa*."

The second thing, of course, was the dancing.

Isabelle had hired a klezmer band called Yid Vicious to serenade our friends and family before the ceremony with peppery tunes like "Tantz, Tantz, Kneydelkh" and "Der Heyser Bulgar," tunes whose titles I could translate (with my slightly improving Yiddish) only as "Dance, Dance, Little Matzo Balls" and "The Heated Bulgarian."

At the reception afterwards, the band, in their outlandish hats and vests, played for all they were worth, while Isabelle and I were lifted onto chairs and wrapped and unwrapped and wrapped again in long streams of crepe paper, with Franny running in and out between everyone's legs, and our guests dancing in two circles beneath us, the women beneath Isabelle, Oona and my sisters and my father's wife, the fringe of her cowgirl suit fly-ing, her large brood of sons holding hands with my father and the other men beneath me, while others of our friends stood on the periphery, electrons to our nuclei, watching and laugh-ing or sipping their wine, their conversations competing with the music and the clattering din of kitchen workers cleaning up the meal.

For me, however, the moment came when Isabelle encircled me.

Several of her friends had warned her against this custom, feeling that it was somehow antifeminist of her, as a bride, to en-circle her groom. At their weddings, they told her, they had done away with the circling or else the bride had encircled the groom and then the groom had encircled the bride.

"That's the only fair way," Mychal Zauberman said at their weekly women's group, and Grace Epstein concurred. At her wedding, Grace told Isabelle, she had lost count of the circling. Feeling dizzy, she had stepped upon her train and fallen. Brac-ing herself against one of the beams of the *chupa,* she toppled everything, and the wine had spilled onto a microphone, creat-ing a small electrical fire, which damaged the paneling on the synagogue's eastern wall, and as a result, the synagogue had sued her. The case was not yet settled, although her marriage had dis-solved many years ago.

Her aversion to the circling, she told Isabelle, had nothing to do with feminism or the demands of modernity, and everything to do with practical reality: the tradition was too hazardous to be risked.

"It's not a commandment," Rabbi Gurwitz sought to reassure a distraught Isabelle, who had wanted as traditional a wedding as possible. "It's merely a custom, my dear, and three short turns should suffice."

Undeterred, however, Isabelle insisted on the full seven rotations. Citing the Kabbalistic writings, which Rabbi Gurwitz had forbidden her to read and which she continued reading nevertheless with Rabbi Falconer, she argued that, unlike the number six, which represents the compass points of empirical reality (the four cardinal directions plus "up" and "down"), the number seven transcends the physical world, representing the still, hidden point of reality inside the beating heart of the cosmos.

Recalling the work she had done as a part-time graduate student in the philosophy of religions, she further placated her postmodernist friends' objections with the syncretistic observation that "It's the same in tantric yoga, where the yoni encircles the lingam," and this, for some reason, was all they needed to hear in order to give her their full support.

FRANNY DROPS HER rose petals down the center aisle and takes her place beneath the *chupa*. Standing against me, she wipes her thumb on her skirts. Her glasses raked, as always, crookedly across her face, she grabs onto my leg and drapes the bottom of my prayer shawl around her shoulders. Peeking out from beneath it, she stares up at the two rabbis.

Rabbi Gurwitz clears his throat and looks meaningfully at Rabbi Falconer. The two of them glance at the floor and reposition their feet. A yearning fiddle finds its voice as Yid Vicious launches into the opening notes of a slow Ladino tune called "Por Qué Llorax la Blanca Niña" (Why Does the Pale Girl Cry). And like a thief, the clarinet steals the melody.

Isabelle enters, radiant in her white dress, walking unescorted down the aisle, a halo of pale tea roses in her hair.

She ascends the few steps to stand beneath the *chupa,* and as she encircles me, gliding around me the requisite seven times, everything slows down, my vision fractures, and I seem to see her from all sides at once. It's as though I were standing inside a perfectly formed circle of light, and an odd feeling wells up inside my chest. I experience a kind of shattering in my heart, which, had I only been another person or myself at another time, I might have recognized as joy.

acknowledgments

Many thanks to the scholars whose work informed my thinking at times in this book: Martin van Amerongen, Daniel Boyarin, Sander L. Gilman, James Hillman, Larry Sullivan; to friends who periodically answered my odd research questions: Dan Appelrouth, Keir Beard, Kim Ben-Porat, Tom Lane, Harold and Karen Goldstein, Dale Nordenberg, Kerry Shale, Bentley Skibell, Mark Southern, Seth Wolitz; to friends and colleagues who read and commented on various drafts: Rick Ehrstin, Hilene Flanzbaum, Maureen Freer, James Magnuson, Eric Richards, Elisabeth Scharlatt, Alex Shakar, Barbara Freer Skibell, Ina Stern, Wendy Weil, Eddy Yanofsky; to Judit Bodnar for her heroic copyediting; to the editorial staff of the *New York Times Sophisticated Traveler* for sending me to Poland and the American Southwest; to the Hambidge Center for a silent and solitary place to work; and to my young nephews, Aaron and Jacob Winston who, when the book was still called *Neuroticism and the Opening Heart in the Song Cycles of Gustav Mahler,* led an informal research group of close relatives in search of a better title.

J.S.